MERCHANTS OF SOULS

TO PAT,

THANKS FOR THE SUPPORT

Earl Lynn 4/25/21

STL

MERCHANTS OF SOULS

BY EARL LYNN

Charleston, SC
www.PalmettoPublishing.com

Paperback ISBN: 978-1-64990-947-3
eBook ISBN: 978-1-64990-674-8

To my wife and friend Cheryl,

THANK YOU! For being who you are.

SUMMARY

THIS IS A STORY OF how two Black women living in Jim Crow Mississippi during the early 1960s meet and discover that they are searching for the same answers as they hunt for the cause of their loved ones' illnesses. What they find will lead them on a journey through the world, between life and the gates of hell. It will be more challenging than either of them could have ever imagined in their wildest dreams. And through it all, their courage to persevere and their ability to continue to love long after hope has been overwhelmed will chaperon them through the darkest hours of the night.

Chapter 1

ON THE WAY HOME

IT IS LATE OCTOBER, AND the year is 1963. The wind makes an eerie noise as it blows through the bright-red, yellow, and orange leaves on the trees that make up the dense dark woods lining both sides of the two-lane road that runs through the center of town. It is the time of year when the air is just starting to get a little chilly during the late hours of the evenings.

Willie has just finished having a few drinks at Cagle's and is getting ready to head home to Coffeeville, where he, his wife, Lynn, and their three children live. Cagle's is a little juke joint that sits on the main street of a town named Charleston.

Charleston is a typical Mississippi town in most ways. It was very small, very rural, and very segregated. It is located about thirty miles off of the main road in a part of the state known as the Delta.

Willie leans his head back as he gulps down the last of his drink. He then pulls a cigarette from the almost-empty pack that he has on the bar and attempts to light it with his cigarette lighter. After several unsuccessful attempts, he bangs the lighter against the edge of the bar so hard that he puts a dent in its outer case. After mumbling a few words of profanity, he tries once more. This time, the flint finally gives off enough sparks to ignite a flame.

I think it's time to buy a new lighter, he thinks as he closes it and sticks it back into his pocket. He then lays a tip on the bar, says his goodbyes to the bartender, and heads for the door.

As he steps out of the door of the tavern, he and a woman collide as she's tries to enter the establishment. The collision knocks the cigarette from his mouth and onto the floor, where it gets stepped on by the woman. Willie looks up at her and immediately becomes tongue-tied, as her stunning appearance commands his undivided attention.

"I am so sorry," she says ...in voice so soft that, if it weren't for Willie staring directly at her face, it would fade into the sound of music and conversation. Realizing that he can hardly hear her, she takes him by the arm and pulls him toward her and whispers her apology once more. Willie gets goosebumps as the hairs on the back of his neck stand up when he feels the warmth from her breath blowing onto his neck and earlobe.

The woman is dressed in a sexy, black, silky-looking dress with a dark-brown mink stole wrapped around her shoulders. Her hair is long and jet black, and it looks as if she has just stepped out of one of those big-city, high-dollar hair salons. And the dress that she is wearing accents every curve on her shapely body.

Her fragrance is soft and yet so appealing that it would make the most sought-after flower envious and any man stop dead in his tracks to take notice. Although it is night, she is wearing dark spectacle-like glasses, which in some bizarre way, add to her mystic beauty, Willie thinks.

"No, excuse me!" Willie says as he starts to pat himself down in search of his pack of cigarettes, still gawking at the alluring female.

"Looking for something?" she asks just as Willie locates his cigarettes and pulls the almost-empty pack from the pocket of his jacket.

"Not anymore. I think I found it. But thanks for asking," he replies as he steps back through the doorway to allow her to enter.

"You're not from around here. Or are you?" he asks.

The woman stops and smiles as Willie holds out the pack of cigarettes and offers her the only one that is left in the pack. As she takes the cigarette, she asks "Why do you ask?"

"No special reason. It's just that I come here all the time, and I have never seen you in here before," Willie answers as he pulls his lighter from his pocket to light her cigarette.

After he flicks the lighter several times, it finally lights.

"I was just thinking to myself a few minutes ago… hmmm…must be time to get a new lighter or at least put some more fluid in this one," he says with a smile. As he starts to pull his hand away, she grabs it in a very seductive fashion and blows out the flame.

"If you would like, I think I know someone that can fix this for you. I'll have them fix it, and I'll give it back to you the next time I see you. What do you say, handsome?" she says as she raises her eyebrows, prompting a "yes" answer.

She then adds, "That would also give me something to look forward to," as she takes the lighter and sticks it down into her black-lace bra.

Willie replies, "Why don't you just keep it? Because I told someone very dear to me that I stopped smoking a long time ago. And besides, that way you will always have something to remember our sweet-yet-brief encounter by." As the smile on his face grows into an almost-cheapish grin, the woman turns and goes about her way.

As she walks off, Willie stares at her buttocks. Her shapely hips move from side to side while she very slowly and deliberately starts to make her way across the room. After a few steps, she stops and turns as if she knows that Willie was watching. She then nods her head and softly blows him a kiss.

After getting into his car, Willie thinks about the woman for another moment or two as he starts the engine and tunes his radio to his favorite late-night blues station. He smiles, thinking to himself, *Yes! I still got the touch*. He then drives off.

While driving down the road, he starts to search through his pockets once more for a cigarette. Being pre-occupied with rummaging for a cigarette and the effect of the alcohol, he momentarily releases the steering wheel. The car swerves and runs onto the shoulder.

As he struggles to regain control, the sound of the gravel hitting the underbody of the car reminds him that he should keep his mind on the road. Because walking the dark roads of Mississippi at night is not how a Black man wants to find himself, drunk or sober.

After driving a few miles, he comes across a dimly lit, two-pump gas station. Willie knows this station well. Mainly because he has passed it on many occasions while on his way to and from his favorite tavern. But this evening, it seems somehow different, Willie thinks to himself. Knowing that he has had a few drinks, he writes it off as the alcohol playing tricks with his mind and causing him to imagine things—as liquor sometimes does.

As he turns onto the lot, he catches a glimpse of what looks like a tiny red light, which appears to be just inside the thick, dark tree line. But it quickly vanishes before he can turn his head to get a better look. As he parks the car, he looks up at the full moon that is shining brightly in the night sky, and he mumbles while slightly shaking his head from side to side, "I really need to cut back on the drinking."

He blows his warm breath through his fists and turns up the collar on his jacket as he is greeted by a small gust of the cold autumn night air while stepping from the car. With the wind, comes the faint aroma of rags, or perhaps burlap, being burned off in a distance. Sometimes, residents burn these items to ward off snakes, which are often associated with the devil or evil spirits. He glances once more into the dark woods, where he saw the light just before walking into the station.

Once inside, he sees the station attendant standing behind the counter, opening cartons of cigarettes and putting the packs into the rack behind the cash register.

"What can I do for you?" the young attendant asks.

"Give me a pack of them humps," Willie replies. Humps are the nickname Willie uses for the brand of filter-less cigarettes that he smokes.

Opening the cigarettes, Willie asks, "What happened to that old guy that worked here?" The attendant replies, "Not really sure. But there was something about him cracking up and having to go to a mental hospital or something like that."

Willie pulls a cigarette from the pack and then reaches for his lighter. Remembering that he gave his lighter to the woman, he asks the attendant for a light. The attendant pulls a small box of matches from behind the counter and hands it to Willie.

After lighting his cigarette, Willie asks for the time. The attendant hands Willie a fancy pocket watch with some engravings on the back.

"I didn't ask for your watch. I just asked for the time!' Willie says as he hands him his watch back.

"No, go ahead. You can keep it," says the attendant.

"I can't do that," says Willie. "From the looks of this fancy thing, it wouldn't be long before you are regretting having given it away. Honestly, I couldn't do that to a hard-working young man like you. Ah…what's your name, son?" Willie smiles and walks toward the door. "David!" the young man replies.

David is a young man who has a lot on his mind this night. Even though their meeting was brief and he was intoxicated, Willie could see that the young man was troubled and was looking for a way to perhaps put some emotional distance between himself and whatever it was that was bothering him.

Chapter 2

DAVID

A FEW DAYS BEFORE DAVID meets Willie, he and his mother are sarcastically discussing him getting a haircut.

"David, do you want to know what you look like with all that hair on your head?" his mother asks.

"No, but I have a strange feeling that you're going to tell me anyway," he replies as he puts on his jacket.

"At least have him cut some of it off. No one's going to hire a walking stick with a cotton ball stuck on the end of it. And don't forget that we're cleaning out the attic when you get back," she says as he walks out the door.

His "Yes, Mother" reply is heard but is muffled by the closed door.

"Are you two at it again?" David's older brother Sonny asks as he walks down the steps, carrying a large box. "He'll grow up one of these days. Just give him some time," he says as he sets the box down on the kitchen floor.

"I know," she replies. "But that boy is so much like his father. I don't know whether I should love him to death or just strangle him."

Sonny jokingly replies, "Please don't strangle him, Mom! Because if you do that, it will leave only me to finish cleaning out the attic, and I've already finished doing my part. And just for the record, this box is the last of my stuff. The rest belongs to you guys. Love you. Got to stop by home before going to work."

Sonny gives his mother a kiss on the cheek, picks up his box, and heads out the door.

Later that evening, David returns home.

"Now that's how a young man looking for a job should look," his mother says, complimenting his new haircut. "Any business should be proud to have such a handsome young man representing them."

"Not only do I look good, but while at the barbershop, I mentioned to Mr. Davis that I was looking for a job, and he told me about a conversation that he had had with one of his customers about a job opening. So, as soon as he finished cutting my hair, I went right over there and applied, and they hired me on the spot. Soo...I found a job!" David says while smiling from ear-to-ear.

"Oh my goodness! A job doing what?" his mother asks.

"At a gas station, and they want me to start as soon as possible. The only bad thing about it is that I got to work the late shift. But the owner said that I can go to days as soon as he finds another person."

David's mother hesitates for a moment as she processes the thought of him working at the gas station late at night. As her mind struggles to come up with something positive to say, her mouth blurs out as if it has a mind of its own, "Alone?"

David replies, "Pretty much. The manager leaves around 6:00 p.m., and I'll be closing it down around 1:00 a.m. The manager says that there are not a lot of customers during those hours, so I'll be doing some cleaning and restocking most of the time."

Sensing his mother's unease with his new place of employment, he attempts to change the conversation. "How much more is left to do in the attic?" he asks.

"Not much. Your brother finished his part. The only thing left is that corner of boxes with your dad's old stuff in them. So, the sooner we get started, the sooner we get done," his mother says as she motions for him to head in that direction.

After sifting through what seems like the last of the boxes, David starts to take several boxes of stuff to the trash. Just as he starts down the stairs, he sees another a box. The box is hidden way back in the corner of the attic behind several stacks of old magazines.

"Mom, what's in this box?" David asks.

"I'm not really sure. We'll need to go through it and find out," she answers as David starts to pull the boxes out to the center of the floor; there is a knock at the door.

David looks at his mom, and she looks back at him, and they both smile. "Ok, I'll get it this time, but the next time, it's your turn. Mr. Man with the new job!" she says as she heads toward the door. At the bottom of the steps, she yells out, "Keep working, we need to finish!"

Chapter 3

THE BEGINNING

WHILE WALKING BACK TO HIS car, Willie shakes his head as he thinks about the young man he just met working at the gas station. However, these thoughts about the young man are interrupted when he sees the tiny red light again. This time, the light seemed closer, and it is moving on a horizontal plane—as if it is not only watching Willie, but following him as well. Once back inside of his car, he scans his surroundings and sees that it has vanished once again.

"I really need to cut back on my drinking," he repeats to himself once more in a low sarcastic voice as he drives off.

As he continues his journey home, thoughts of the strange light stick in his head. But what bothers him even more than seeing the light is trying to figuring out what was different about the gas station—other than the original attendant not being there. By the time he turns onto the road that leads up to his house, thoughts of what he experienced have faded.

Willie steps out of his car and leans back against it as he steadies himself in preparation for the walk up the steps of the porch to the front door. Prior to starting his journey, he looks down the street, which is pitch-dark other than a tiny red light off in the far distance. Unlike the lights that he saw earlier, this light is headed straight in his direction.

As the light gets nearer, Willie takes a deep breath and slowly exhales. He scrunches his eyes as he vaguely starts to see a shape of sort start to become visible around the light. Once the shadowy figure steps into the dim ray of light shining from the window of the front room of the house, Willie releases a sigh of relief. Its his neighbor, Amos Koons.

"What are you doing standing out here at this time of night?" Amos asks as he and his dog walks by. "Willie, while still trying to get over the fright, replies "Just trying to get a little fresh air.". Amos Koons is the only White person that lives in the neighborhood.

After navigating the stairs, he walks into the house and kisses his wife, Lynn, on the lips and says to her, "I am so happy to have you. Love of my life!" It's just like he has done every night for the past fifteen years—after being out drinking. Lynn returns the pleasantries and helps him undress for bed.

The next morning is the beginning of the weekend, and Willie doesn't work weekends, so he and Lynn get to sleep in. As the sun starts to cast its rays of light through the bedroom curtains, Willie lies in bed with his eyes wide open, not moving a muscle. After a while, Lynn starts to move and eventually wakes up.

She rolls over and puts her arm across Willie's waist and starts to rub his stomach. She then slowly places one of her legs over his and begins to nibble on his ear lobes while whispering her desire to make love to her husband in a soft, low voice.

She eases her hand down Willie's body and into his underwear, where she notices that he isn't getting excited. As a matter of fact, he has not moved a muscle throughout the whole seductive encounter. Lynn rises in the bed and looks at Willie.

What she sees is Willie lying there with both eyes wide open as if he is awake. She then, in a nervous and crackly voice, calls out his name several times. But he still doesn't answer. After giving him several hard shakes without getting any reaction, she starts to scream for help. The older children hear their mother's cry and come running into the bedroom. Lynn grabs her housecoat and runs to call for help.

Chapter 4

THE MEETING

ALMOST A YEAR LATER, WILLIE lies motionless in a hospital in Jackson. Lynn is standing next to his bed, looking out of the window. She crosses her arms and leans up against the wall and then turns her head and looks out the window at the massive park across the street.

She watches as a horse-drawn carriage makes its way through the traffic and turns into the park. The carriage then travels down the cobblestone path that runs through the park until it vanishes into the morning mist. As she stares out at one of the large open fields, she imagines how beautiful it must be during the summer months with its towering trees and possibly many blooming flowers. She then starts to reminisce about the good and bad times that she and her husband have shared through the years.

How in the world will I and the children make it? replays itself over and over again in her mind. After all, Willie has been the breadwinner for as long as they have been together. And just the thought of Willie not being there for her is something she just cannot accept.

She looks over at their youngest child, and her eyes start to fill with tears at the thought of her growing up without her father—whom she loves so very dearly. And even though her heart is heavily burdened with the dim prospects of their future, she knows that she has to continue to be strong if the family is going to survive the even tougher times that are sure to come.

Her thoughts are interrupted when she hears two people talking just outside the room. She can tell from the sound of the voices that they are two men.

One man says, "I know that your father is a big man here in, Jackson, and I also know that you would like to pick or choose your own workload, if you know what I mean? But as long as I am the director of this hospital, you will do and see whomever I tell you to. That is, if you have any plans of continuing your employment here. Now have a good day, doctor!" She then hears footsteps as one of the men walks down the hall.

Willie's doctor walks into the room. His face is red as a beet with an expression of almost complete and utter disgust on it. He stands there, not saying a word, breathing heavily as if someone just chased him down the hall. After a period of complete silence, he clears his throat and starts to speak. As he explains the results of the latest round of medical tests to Lynn and Willie's older brother, Howard, they both listen in hopes that there will be some good news.

Howard and his wife, Morgan, live in Jackson and insisted that Lynn bring Willie there for treatment so that they could do whatever they could to help out.

The doctor goes on to explain how he and his colleagues cannot find anything physically wrong with Willie and that all the tests indicate that his brain is still very active, to the best of their knowledge. Lynn can tell from the look on his face and his body language that he isn't happy about having a Negro as a patient. He probably thinks it is entirely beneath him and a waste of his talents. But still, with her eyes red from crying, she asks in a nervous voice, "So, what is our next move?"

After quickly flipping through the pages on Willie's chart, he answers brusquely, "The hospital is having a staff meeting this afternoon. Your husband's case and a case very similar to his are going to be the topic of the discussions. I'll know more after the meeting!" He then pulls a piece of paper from the clipboard and hands it to Lynn.

"You need to fill out this form and give it to the nurse. We will need it back before any more tests can be run," he explains.

As Lynn fumbles around in her purse in search of a pen, the doctor pulls one from the top pocket of his white coat and hands it to her; he then turns and starts to walk away.

"What should I do with your pen once I'm done with it?" Lynn asks.

"Just keep it!" he snaps as he continues to walk down the hall.

Lynn just stands there for a moment, staring into space.

"Lynn, are you all right?" asks Howard as he put his arms around her and tries and comfort her.

"I'm Ok," she answers after wiping a tear from her face. She then goes into the waiting room and tries and pull herself together.

While in the waiting room, she sees a young Black man sitting across the room reading a newspaper. The man looks up and nods his head to acknowledge her presence. After a while, an older Black woman walks into the room and joins him. Lynn notices that the woman is very well dressed and is wearing a lot of expensive jewelry. Her hair is gray but very nicely done. And when she speaks, it is evident that she is educated. Lynn also can see that she is upset and has been crying as well.

The man and the woman have a brief conversation, then the man stands up and walks out of the room and heads toward the rooms where the patients are kept. The woman looks over at Lynn and sees that she has been crying as well. She then says in a voice loud enough for Lynn to hear from across the room, "Sure looks like there is a lot of pain in this room."

Lynn chuckles, nodding her head in agreement, and then introduces herself.

"Nice to meet you. My name is Madeline Lewis," the woman replies.

Before long, the two women are telling each other about the chain of events that caused their paths to cross. Madeline explains that, about a year ago, her youngest son David came home after working the late shift at a gas station where he had been employed for about a week. "I remember lying in my bed and hearing him come into the house at around two in the morning, as he had always done when he worked that dreadful night shift," she explains.

"The next morning, when I got up, I noticed that he had left the front door unlocked. I went to his room and knocked on his door to ask why, he didn't answer. When I got no response, I opened his door and saw him lying there with his eyes wide open. I tried to get him to respond, but he just laid there. And now, here we are. And what hurts the most is remembering that the last words that we spoke to each other were word spoken out of anger."

By the time Madeline has finished telling her story, Lynn's mouth is wide open. "Where is this gas station located?" Lynn asks.

"On the road between Charleston and Coffeeville. Why do you ask?" Madeline replies.

Lynn tells Madeline what happened to Willie, and at that moment, both women know that the answers to what happened to their loved ones that tragic night lie somewhere on the stretch of road between Charleston and Coffeeville. And they intend to find out just what the answers are.

They both agree that, in two days, on a Saturday, they will meet up at Lynn's house and start their search for the answers.

Chapter 5

THE SEARCH

MADELINE ARRIVES AT LYNN'S HOUSE early. As she walks up to the door, she sees an opening in the curtains that cover the front window. As she peeps through the opening, she sees Lynn kneeling and praying. Madeline bows her head and whispers a short prayer and then waits until she sees that Lynn is finished before knocking on the door.

Lynn opens the door, invites her in, and offers her a seat and a cup of coffee.

Madeline responds, "I'll pass on the seat, but a cup of coffee with two teaspoons of sugar and some cream to go would be nice."

Lynn can see that Madeline is as itching to get started as she is. While Lynn pours two cups of coffee, the two ladies discuss and agree that Lynn should drive, since she is most familiar with the back roads in the area. They will start their search at the gas station.

While walking to the car, Lynn stops, turns around, and runs back into the house as if she forgot something. When she returns, Madeline sees that she is carrying a black leather pouch. "So, what's in the pouch?" Madeline asks.

Lynn replies, "Uncle Leroy."

"Uncle who?" Madeline asks in a puzzled voice.

Lynn repeats, "Uncle Leroy," as she pulls a shiny .357 magnum pistol from the pouch.

The two ladies sit silently as they drive down the curvy, two-lane road toward the gas station. Once they arrive, they see that the station has gone out of business and that weeds have grown up through the cracks in the drive around the pumps. They also notice that the front windows have been broken and that someone has nailed some boards over the front door.

Lynn opens the trunk of the car, pulls out the jack iron, and starts removing the boards from the entrance of the building.

Standing behind her, Madeline asks, "So, why do you call your gun Uncle Leroy?"

"It's a long story, but I'll give you the short version of it. My Great Aunt Laurinda was married to a man named Leroy. She caught him cheating on her with another woman."

"And?" asks Madeline.

"And what?" replies Lynn.

"Oh!" Madeline says.

Once inside, Lynn attempts to turn on the lights and finds that the electricity to the building has been turned off as well. While Lynn holds the door open to allow the light to come in, Madeline digs around in her purse for her cigarette lighter.

With the flickering flame from the lighter illuminating their path, the two ladies walk into the old gas station. Once inside, they smell the aroma of mildew and hear the sounds of water dripping onto something made of metal. Each drip of the water echoes through the building like an amplified tick from a cheap clock. They see paper scattered all about the place and standing puddles of water on the floor from the leaks in the roof.

As they progress farther into the building, Lynn sees traces of daylight streaming from behind a stack of empty boxes. She walks over and kicks the boxes out from against the wall and sees a small opening in the wall.

"Someone has been living in here," she says as the sunlight from the opening partly lights up that section of the building. While Lynn is looking at the opening in the wall, Madeline sees a door that looks as if it leads to a back room. She looks over at Lynn and motions for her to come over and check it out. After making their way over to the door, Madeline reaches out and grabs the doorknob and starts to turn it.

Just as the knob starts to turn, something grabs it from the other side. Madeline quickly releases it and steps back. They hear a loud, blood-curdling scream coming from the other side of the door. Both ladies panic and start to run toward the exit. In their haste, they become entangled and trip over one another and fall to the floor. Lynn reaches for the pistol and realizes that she forgot to put it in her pocket after showing it to Madeline earlier.

As they scramble to get back on their feet, they hear a loud crash, accompanied by the sound of breaking glass, which is followed by another loud scream. But this time, the scream sounds as if it is heading away from the building. After making it back through the front door, Lynn runs to the car and grabs the pistol.

"Madeline! Stay behind me," she shouts as they slowly work their way toward the back of the building.

Once around back, they see that the back window has been knocked out and that several bloody footprints are leading from the building and into the woods. Lynn holds the shiny pistol out in front of her as they follow the trail of blood into the dark woods. Both of them have second thoughts about going into the woods, but they keep them to themselves because they know that this could be that one missing piece of the puzzle.

As they walk into the thick brush, the canopy from the tall trees blocks out the rays from the sun. At first, it seems really dark, and they can only make out the shapes of the large trees. But after a while, their eyes adjust to the change in light, and they can see that the trail of blood leads to a path that goes even deeper into the shadowy forest.

While making their way down the path, they notice the faint odor of something burning off in the distance and a repeated childlike whimper coming from the injured "whatever it is that they are chasing."

Madeline calls out, "Hey! Please don't run from us! We will help you!"

22

But the wounded entity never replies and continues to remain just out of sight. And as the trail of blood becomes almost constant, the ladies press their pursuit.

Soon, the narrow path starts to widen and then ends at a field of tall grass. They can see the tall grass give way as the whimpering creature make its way across. Lynn looks up at the skyline and sees smoke coming from the chimney of a shack that's located near the tree line on the other side of the field.

"Why don't we stop for a moment and rest," Lynn says as she stops and puts her hand on her hips. While they are catching their breath, she points to the smoke. Madeline looks up, rubs her hair back out of her face, and says, "Looks like our friend might be heading home."

Chapter 6

UNWANTED GUESTS

WALKING UP TO THE SHACK, they notice that someone has hung old burlap potato sacks with holes in them up to the windows so that no one can see inside. The wood that the shack is made of is starting to rot and break away due to many years of not being painted or replaced. The yard around the cabin is a mixture of mostly crabgrass and gravel, and the roof is made of tin. On the front porch are two chairs padded with old patched quilts and a couple of old empty coffee containers sitting on the floor between them. Strangest of all is that there is no road leading to or from the property.

Lynn steps onto the front porch. She hears someone from inside the house ask in an inquisitive and crumbling voice, "Who's there?"

Lynn replies, "Lynn," in a voice she thinks is loud enough for the person inside the house to hear. The door slowly opens. The person on the other side partly exposes himself and repeats the question. "*Who's there?*"

This time, the question is asked in a louder tone and in a more direct fashion.

Lynn repeats her response. But in a lower and somewhat humbler tone, as she covertly sticks the pistol back into her pocket and steps down off of the porch. Slowly, the door opens wider.

Once it is fully open, an old woman steps out of the shadows of the dark interior and partly into the daylight. Lynn and Madeline both look on in almost complete shock.

They both try not to show any reaction at all, which makes them seem afraid. And being afraid is precisely the reaction that Lynn and Madeline do not want to display. But they are so startled that they can't do anything but stand there and gape at the strange-looking old lady. Neither of them move an inch for several seemingly endless moments.

Standing motionless in the front yard, they stare at the old lady as if she is something neither of them have ever seen—or for that matter, could imagine in their scariest dreams.

The skin on the woman's face looks to be well over a hundred years old. She has long, frizzy white hair and long curled fingernails. Her hands are disfigured from years of arthritis, and she has a patch over her left eye. The right eye is covered with a cataract that is so severe, the iris looks almost white from where Lynn is standing. She is hunched over and walks with a very strange-looking cane.

"What can I do for you ladies?" the old woman asks.

"How do you do, Miss? My name is Lynn, and this here is my friend Madeline," Lynn says. The old lady hesitates for a second, tilting her head while straining to make out their faces. "My name is Althea. What is it that you want?"

"We are looking for someone that might have come this way," Lynn answers.

"What does he or she look like?" asks the woman.

"I can't really answer that. All we know is that they are losing a lot of blood and that they were last seen heading in this direction," Lynn responds.

The old woman pauses for a moment as she peeks around Lynn to get a better look at Madeline. She then replies in an angry voice, "No! I haven't seen or heard a thing all day! Now, get off my property before I call the sheriff!"

As Lynn and Madeline walk back toward the field of tall grass that all but surrounds the old shack, they both can tell that the old woman is hiding something.

As soon as they know that they are out of sight, they circle around and come up from the back side of the shack and hide in the tall grass at the edge of the clearing. After a while, the old woman steps out of the back door of the cabin and heads toward a shed. She looks around as if making sure that no one is watching. She then uses her strange-looking cane to hobble over to the door of a shed, which is located in the back of the cabin about thirty yards away. The shed is also in bad need of repair. The roof is made of tin, and there are several broken and missing boards on the sides of the structure.

The door has only one hinge that holds it on, so the old woman has to lift it a little to open it. This is the only other structure on the property, other than an old outhouse. Lynn and Madeline watch as the old woman makes several trips to and from the shed, carrying bundles under her arms. After the fourth trip, the old woman starts to get tired and sits down on the steps that lead to the back door of the shack. She then gazes up at the bright sun which has started its descent, and rests her head against the back door. Soon, she nods off into a deep sleep.

After seeing the old woman nod off, Lynn and Madeline ease their way out of the dense grass and toward the shack. Once they've made it to the shed, Madeline slowly opens the door as Lynn keeps a sharp eye on the old woman. They can see that the trail of blood leads right up to the shed and continues on inside. They both take a deep breath, and Lynn places her hand inside her jacket pocket that contains the pistol. Once inside, they see several lanterns sitting on the ground next to the door.

Lynn picks up one of the lanterns, lights it, and turns up the flame. As the light from the lamp gets brighter, the ladies can see that what they thought was a shed is actually a structure concealing the steps leading down into the earth. After reaching the bottom of the steps, they find themselves at the entrance of an underground tunnel.

The tunnel is about twenty feet underground and has a ceiling that is about six feet high. The walls are about five feet apart, and it is cold, damp, and very dark. Someone scattered pieces of wood on the floor to cover the holes that are made from puddles of standing water softening the soil and allowing it to wash away. Lynn wraps her fingers around the handle of the pistol, and Madeline clutches her forearm.

With the lantern held out in front of them, they are able to look up and see the roots covered with cobwebs and intertwined with the soil to form the rough-looking ceiling of the passageway. The wind hums as it blows through the cracks that are in and around the door at the top of the steps. Lynn starts to ask Madeline something but is shushed before she can complete her sentence.

Madeline whispers in a shallow voice, "Look." She points toward a dim light that is deep inside of the tunnel. It looks like the type of light that would come from a small lantern or perhaps a single candle.

As the two women inch away from the stairs and toward the light, they spot the silhouette of something moving about in the area where the light is illuminating from. As the erratic shadows bounce about the walls, it send their imaginations running to the worst of places. Lynn pulls the pistol from her pocket as she continues to cautiously make her way forward. With their backs against the wall, Lynn peeks out of the shadows and sees that the narrow corridor opens up into a reasonably large cave.

She passes the lantern to Madeline and raises the pistol to the firing position. Madeline adjusts the flame in the lamp down as low as she can without putting it out. They then move along the wall to the edge of the opening. Her heart throbbing from an intense mixture of emotions and fear, Madeline slowly pokes her head around the corner and looks into the cavern.

Her anxiety is greatly diminished as she sees a moth flying around a single candle sitting on a altar near the center of the cavern. The light emitting from the small flickering flame makes the moth's shadow look as if it is ten feet tall. And as the shadow dances around the walls and ceiling, it adds to the already eerie ambiance in the damp and dark cavity in the earth.

The cave has several rows of shelves dug into its walls at various heights, and an old rickety ladder leans against the wall. Sitting on the shelves are an assortment of different-sized and colored jars. They can tell that some of the jars have been sitting in the same location for a long, long time from the thickness of the cobwebs that cover them.

The cave also houses a sizable makeshift altar, which is located near the center of the space, and a single chair, which is sitting next to a door that is located on the far side of the chamber. The door has a small opening near its upper center with several strings of barbed wire nailed across it. It also has a large brass deadbolt lock on it, which allows it to be locked from the outside.

There are several large candles placed in various places around the cavern that, when lit, illuminate the area around the altar. The ceiling is about twelve or thirteen feet high, with cobwebs and large roots dangling from it. As Lynn looks at the size of the roots and the thickness of the layers of cobwebs, she thinks, *This cavern must be hundreds of years old.*

Looking around the room, Madeline takes notice of the numerous various jars lining the dirt shelves. The first jar that she looks at contains a necklace and some white powder. The second jar contains a ring and some more white powder.

And as she continues to look, she notices that each and every jar contains only one item, along with a small quantity of the white powder. There is one with a cigarette lighter in it, another with a small child's toy, and then another that contains a comb—and so on.

While Madeline is looking at the jars, Lynn raises the lantern so that she can look through the opening in the door. She then releases a loud gasp as she sees what is on the other side. Madeline quickly turns her head in Lynn's direction when she hears the sound.

"What is it?" she asks in a frantic voice. Lynn can hardly get a word out. Then finally, she responds, "You got to see this!"

What she sees is a frail, almost childlike creature lying in the corner of the closed off room on a bed of rags. The creature has the face of an old man with eyes as black as night. Its body—except for its hands, feet, and the area around its face—is covered with a type of coarse hair.

The hair is like that of a wild boar or a grizzly bear. It bares its sharp canine teeth and makes a serpent-like hissing sound as it looks into Lynn's face. Lynn can tell right off that this is the same creature that they have been following since they left the gas station—because of the open wound on its face and upper body. She can also tell from the bloody rags that are lying on the floor that the old woman has been doctoring it.

Still staring at the creature, she calls to Madeline once more: "You need to see this." Madeline replies, "No! You need to see this."

Lynn slowly backs away from the door toward where Madeline is standing and holds the lantern up so that she can see what Madeline is looking at.

In one of the jars is a gold-plated pocket watch with an inscription on its cover that reads, "To David. With love, Dad."

"That belonged to my David," says Madeline as tears start to roll down her cheeks. "How did it get down here?"

In an attempt to comfort her, Lynn puts her arm around her.

While the two ladies are embracing, they hear the echo of a loud bang and immediately know what it was. It was from the door at the top of the steps, and it sounds like someone slammed it shut. Lynn looks down the tunnel and sees a light coming in their direction. She quickly puts out the lantern, and both ladies hide behind the altar.

Soon, a young woman with long dark hair walks into the chamber. She is carrying a burning lantern in one hand and a bundle of rags and a stick in the other. Lynn and Madeline both can see that the woman has a patch over one of her eyes and that her cane is actually the same strange-looking cane that the old woman had when they met her at the front door of the shack. The woman chants what sounds like a spell of a sort as she walks up to the door of the closed-off room that houses the wounded creature.

Lynn now knows that they must do something before the lady opens the door because the creature inside saw her and she has no idea what its reaction will be once the door opens.

She whispers to Madeline, "As soon as she opens that door, run for the exit. Don't worry. I will be right behind you."

She then takes Madeline by the hand and squeezes it as if to tell her, "Don't be afraid; be strong."

The woman gradually opens the door while staring the beast in the eyes and repeating the chant over and over again. As soon as the door is open wide enough, Lynn yells out to Madeline, "Run!" She jumps out from behind the altar, pushes the woman into the room with the creature, and slams the door shut before the woman can catch on to what is happening.

Madeline runs through the tunnel as fast as her feet can carry her. As she is running, she hears snarling and growling sounds coming from inside the cavern behind her. The ungodly noises are followed by five gunshots and then several loud screams. As the screams echo through the tunnel, Madeline's heart beats faster and faster. She navigates her way back toward the entrance.

Then all at once, there is dead silence. It is so quiet that Madeline can hear herself gasp as she stops to catch her breath and get her bearings back.

"I need to go back and help Lynn," she ponders. And as she starts to turn around to go back, the silence is broken. The sound is faint at first, but then it becomes louder and louder.

The once-faint sound suddenly become clear. There are footsteps, and they are rapidly moving in her direction. And whoever—or whatever—it is it is really in a big hurry. Not knowing if the footsteps belong to Lynn or to the other woman, she turns back around and starts running toward the exit even faster than before. As the footsteps get closer, Madeline turns her head to look back over her shoulder.

While looking back, she trips over one of the boards lying on the ground and falls face down in the mud. During the fall, she twists her ankle and cut her face just below her right eye. As she scuffles to get back on her feet, Lynn comes running up from behind. The tunnel is so dark and Lynn is running so fast that she doesn't see Madeline lying on the floor until it is too late. Lynn comes crashing down on top of her.

As both ladies struggle to get to their feet, they start hearing the screams once more. But now they are louder and practically right on top of them. Madeline wipes the mud from her face as she looks down the dark tunnel in the direction from which they've come.

A tiny light suddenly appears almost out of thin air. Its glow is insignificant in size, yet its glow is so mesmerizing that she finds it nearly impossible to take her eyes off of it. The hypnotic light paralyzes Madeline to the point that she cannot move a muscle; she just stands there, watching it as it comes closer.

Lynn shouts out to Madeline, "Get up and run!"

But she doesn't move a muscle. She just keeps staring at the light. Once the light gets close enough, Lynn then sees what it really is. It is the once-beautiful young lady, and she has transformed into a hideous creature.

This creature has the tongue of a serpent and two large eyes. One eye is covered with a milky, white-colored layer of skin, and the other glistens like a ruby. Her hair is white and flowing in all different directions as she makes a blood-curdling screaming sound that is intermittently replaced by a loud, serpent-like hiss.

The joints of her body have the ability to rotate and fold in either direction, which allows her to move from the floor to the walls and then to the ceiling of the tunnel like an insect, all while seemingly exerting little or no effort. And like a giant insect advancing on its prey, she moves in on the women as Lynn scuffles about on the muddy floor, trying to get to her feet.

The hideous creature takes Madeline by the arm and starts to drag her back down into the tunnel. Madeline goes almost willingly, still in her mesmerized state. Lynn makes it to her feet and runs up the steps and pushes the door open in her attempt to escape. The opened door allows the rays from the setting sun to shine directly down into the tunnel and onto the devilish beast. As soon as the creature is touched by the light from the sun, it screams out as if it had been dowsed with a pan of boiling hot water. And it quickly releases Madeline's arm and vanishes deep into the tunnel.

Lynn runs back down the steps and grabs Madeline by the hand and drags her up the steps and out the door. Once outside, Madeline quickly awakens from the spell. They then hurry across the field of tall grass to the path that leads back to the gas station. Neither of them can believe what they have seen with their very own eyes. As they walk some and run some, Lynn keeps a close watch on the sun as it sinks down behind the trees and the day turns into evening.

Chapter 7

THE STRANGER

With the last of the sun's rays disappearing beneath the horizon, the leaves on the towering trees seem to slowly turn in their attempt to capture the last bits of the day's light. And while the branches sway ever so slightly from the slightest of wind, the many shadows from the forest's persona start to dance about on the leaf-covered floor as Lynn and Madeline, with their eyes scanning and their hearts throbbing, hurry toward the gas station.

As the sun vanishes and the dancing shadows are replaced by still darkness, the whiff of burning burlap once again touches the night air. Sounds from the creatures of the forest moving about as they prepare themselves for the night become more and more prevalent as the night gradually starts to take hold.

"Are you sure this is the way back to the gas station?" asks Madeline.

"Yes! I'm sure, but if I wasn't sure, what would you want to do? Go back where we came from?" answers Lynn.

After a short silence, Madeline whispers, "I sure hope that you still got some bullets in that gun." She gazes at a large shadow that is coming through the trees.

Lynn answers, "One, maybe. Why do you ask?"

Madeline squeezes Lynn's forearm ever so slightly as she pulls her around to get her to look in the direction of the strange-looking profile. Lynn slowly pulls the pistol from her pocket as they both stop and stand still in their tracks.

As the shadow gets closer, the ladies can see that it is a middle-aged Black man with a heavy mustache and beard. He is dressed in hunting gear and carrying a shotgun. Lynn eases the pistol back into her pocket but keeps her finger on the trigger as the stranger steps onto the path about twenty-five feet in front of them.

As he gets closer, he appears to see the mud on their clothes, the cut on Madeline's face, and the noticeable limp in her walk.

"What are you two doing out here?" the man asks.

"Trying to find our way out," Lynn quickly replies as if it was a rhetorical question.

"My name is Madeline, and this is my friend Lynn, and we're lost," Madeline blurts out before Lynn can stop her.

"We're not lost!" Lynn says as she points to the place where they entered onto the path near the back of the station.

"I once had a friend a long, long time ago who had a daughter named Mary Lynn. She was a cute little something that always asked a lot of questions. My wife and I was very fond of her and wanted to have a daughter just like her someday. But I guess it just wasn't meant to be," the man says as he reminisces and tries and ease their fear of running into a strange man in the forest.

"Mary Lynn is a common name in the south. It was my grandmother's name as well," Lynn says as she starts to let down her defenses just a little bit.

"What in the world happened to you two?" the stranger asks curiously . The ladies want to tell him right away about what happened, but they cannot believe the chain of events, nor do they know where to begin.

After a moment or two, Lynn says, "You wouldn't believe it if we told you."

"Try me," the stranger replies.

So, as the man walks with them, they attempt to explain to him what they both saw and experienced. After a while, Madeline starts to notice how the man gazes at Lynn as if she somehow looks familiar to him—but when she looks in his direction, he looks away. As he listens to what they have to say, he hardly says a word and he seems unsurprised at what they're saying. She also notices his nonverbal cues and lack of astonishment and figures that he is questioning the facts of their story. But they know that even they would have a hard time believing it if they hadn't lived it.

They manage to finish the weird tale just as they make it back to their car. Lynn walks around the vehicle to the driver's side and unlocks the door while Madeline thanks the stranger for escorting them. The man then walks around to the car to where Lynn is sitting and asks her for something to write with. She pulls a pen from her purse and hands it to the stranger.

Madeline notices a strange-looking tattoo on his forearm as he reaches out for the pen. The stranger then pulls a small piece of paper from his pocket and writes a phone number on it. "If I can be of any help to either of you, just give me a call the next time you are heading out this way. I'll be heading on in as well before my wife Irene starts looking for me. You all take care now."

As the ladies start to drive off, Madeline asks Lynn to stop the car. Madeline rolls down the window and yells out to the stranger, "Hey! Didn't you forget something?"

The man looks back with a startled expression. After thinking for a moment, he asks, "What did I forget?"

Madeline replies, with a huge smile on her face, "To return my friend's pen."

The stranger then walks back over to the car and winks as he gives Madeline the pen. He then walks back into the woods as they drive away.

After making it back to Lynn's house, they both agree that no one would believe their story without any hard evidence, especially the police. So, they decide to wait until the next day before making a decision about whether or not they should tell anyone else about what happened. They say their goodbyes, and Madeline heads home.

Once alone, Lynn starts heating water for a bath and pours herself a glass of milk. While waiting for the water to begin boiling, she sits on the couch and picks up a book lying on the table. It is a book that she has been trying to finish for months. She thinks to herself, *Maybe a little reading would help get my mind off the crazy day that I've had.*

After only a short while, she nods off into a deep sleep. And as the water boils, her mind takes her to a place that she has never been before. This place is as real as any place she has ever been while awake. She finds herself standing in the middle of an open field wearing a long beautiful gown.

As she slowly turns, her gown flows in the soothing breeze. And as she looks out, she notices not only how large the field is, but also a massive tree that stands not too far from where she is standing. The area is seemingly endless, except for the one gigantic tree. While she surveys the massive work of Mother Nature, a shadowy figure appears standing beneath it.

The figure stands partly behind the draping branches as if it is trying to hide from her view. And in this dream, she is not afraid of this unknown entity but, in some strange way, attracted to it.

The last of the water boils away, and the pot starts to smoke. While still in this dream, Lynn tries desperately to make out who or what is lurking in the shadows of the tree branches. And as the smoke from the empty pot slowly makes its way into the room where she is sleeping and starts to surround her, she begins to cough ever so slightly—but not enough to awaken her from her deep slumber.

The strange figure in the dream suddenly vanishes with a loud "bang!" It is as if it and the tree became one. The sudden bang not only frightens Lynn in her dream, but it also wakes her up. Coughing, eyes stinging from the smoke, she runs into the kitchen and removes the pot from the stove and tosses it into the sink.

She raises one of the windows to let the smoke out the house. As she steps away from the window, there is another loud "bang!" She sits back down on the side of the bed and rubs her forehead as she recognizes the banging noise. "Good thing Willie never got around to fixing the shutter on that back window" she mutters to herself.

Early the next morning, Lynn calls Madeline. And after talking for only a few minutes, Lynn started to yawn.

"Sounds like your sleepy?" asks Madeline.

"Girl, I know that I went to sleep last night because I left a pot on the stove and almost burned down the house. But what's even stranger is this weird dream that I had. Now, I feel as if I've not slept all night," she says.

"Pretty much the same thing happened to me," Madeline replies. "I just kept tossing and turning after seemingly lying awake until about 4:00 a.m. And with the little sleep that I did get, I kept having this horrible dream about that vile creature standing at the foot of my bed watching over me while repeating some strange chant or something."

"The dream that I had was a strange one as well, but there are some parts of it that I didn't really understand," Lynn further explains.

"There are some really crazy things going on around here," says Lynn as she starts to brush her hair.

"So, what's our next move?" asks Madeline as she quickly changes the subject.

"I need to drive down to Jackson to visit Willie and check on the kids. They are staying with their uncle and aunt until I can get things worked out here. I should be back late Sunday night, and I'm taking some time off from the diner next week. So, I'll give you a call on Monday morning." Lynn answers.

Chapter 8

A GRANDMOTHER'S TALES

As SHE DRIVES DOWN THE highway, many things past through Lynn's mind. She thinks about her husband, Willie, their children, and the things that happened the day before. She also has thoughts of her childhood and the stories that her grandmother would tell her about haunting and ghosts. Lynn had thought her grandmother was superstitious or just trying to frighten her and her siblings, so she didn't put much stock in them.

She then remembers something that her grandmother said while telling one of her many stories. It was about a lady that lived down on the other side of the creek, which was not too far from the town of Charleston. Most of the people around those parts at that time genuinely believe that the woman was not only as old as the creek itself, but also a witch or maybe a specter of some kind.

This belief was perpetuated because the old woman kept to herself and had a dying love for her numerous cats. And, because of the tales of her ability to casts spells on persons or things. These chronicles had been repeatedly told over the years, so many times that some locals would swear that they were fact, even though there was probably no one still alive who had actually seen or witnessed her perform any of the alleged acts. It was still common knowledge in those parts that she was indeed of the unholy.

Lynn then recalls something that her grandmother said that she had witnessed when she was sixteen years old. It was something that she had never told a soul about, other than Lynn. She said, "There was once a young couple that lived not too far from the farm that I grew up on. This couple was so in love that one only had to see them together once to know that it was the kind of love that would last forever if life's longevity was to allow. This couple went almost everywhere and did almost everything together. They truly loved and cared for each other with all of their hearts and souls.

"One late autumn day, while the man was away, something happened, and their barn caught fire. The woman tried to put out the fire, but it grew too rapidly, and soon most of the structure was engulfed in flames. After she saw that she wouldn't be able to extinguish it, she swung open the barn door to retrieve the livestock from inside of the burning structure. As soon as the door opened, the animals came rushing out and stampeded over her.

"When the man returned home later that night, he found her broken body lying in front of the burned-out barn. He rushed her to the doctor as fast as his horse and wagon could carry them, but his beloved soul mate's injuries proved to be fatal, and she died before he could get her there. He felt as if he had lost his only reason for living.

"A day or so later, Papa, Mama, and I went to take him some food as he, and seemingly the whole Negro community, grieved the loss of his wife. When we arrived, Papa knocked on the door, and the man replied, 'Just a moment.' While Papa waited for him to answer the door, I saw the prettiest little kitten that I had ever seen. It had come from under the house. As I went to pet it, it ran to the side of the house, so I followed.

"While in pursuit of the kitten, I heard two people talking. I turned to the direction where the voices were coming from and saw that I was standing next to a window and could see who was talking. It was the man talking to an old woman. As I continued to watch through the window, I saw the man give the old woman his wedding ring, and then he let her out the back door of the house.

"Early one morning, about two weeks after the funeral, Papa sent me out across the pasture to fetch the cows so that they could be milked. I thought that was strange because the cows usually would be at the gate, waiting for the bucket grain that Papa would give them just before milking them. But for some reason, that morning they didn't show up. Papa thought that they might have gotten out during the night, so he went to saddle his horse so that he could go look for them.

"While walking across the damp, dew-covered pasture, I saw something moving about. It was off at a distance, among the sporadic patches of fog. At first, I thought it was the cows or maybe some deer. But it was neither. As I struggled to try and make out what it was, I walked closer.

"It was then that I saw two people walking. They were still off in the distance. So at first, I couldn't tell who they were. But as I got closer, I saw. It was the man and his wife. They were as plain as the nose on my face.

"They were in the meadow walking, talking, laughing, and holding hands. I froze dead in my tracks as I watched them fade away among the clouds of fog. No one has ever seen or heard from the man since.

"Now, some people say he up and moved away because living here was a constant reminder of her. Then, there are others that say he killed himself and no one has ever found the body. But I think they're both wrong. I think that he gave away his soul in exchange for one more moment with the woman that he loved so dearly."

Her grandmother went on to say, "I am not going to tell you that the woman is or is not a witch because I don't really know, but I do believe that some things are best left to the Lord's doing."

As Lynn continues to drive, she comes upon a bus loaded with people traveling in the opposite direction on the highway. She notices that the people on the bus are both White and Black and that they are sitting next to one another—instead of the Blacks sitting in the back. She also notices the sign that one of the riders holds up to the window as she passes them. In large letters, it reads "Right to Vote!"

Chapter 9

DOCTOR IN CHARGE

LYNN ARRIVES AT HER BROTHER-IN-LAW's house, where she is greeted with hugs and kisses from her children. The hugs and kisses are followed by questions about when they are going to go back home. Lynn smiles and answers, "Soon. Very soon."

Howard can see it in her eyes that something was wrong, but he decides that he will wait until they are alone before he asks her about it. After the children finish their hellos, everybody packs into the car, and they drive to the hospital to visit Willie.

Once at the hospital, Lynn and Howard stand in the hall and talk with the doctor about Willie's condition while the children sit in the room on and around the foot of his bed. They sit and watch over him as if, at any moment, he might get right up out of that bed and go home with them, making life beautiful once more.

As they watch over his lifeless body, they talk about all of the fun things that they are going to do once their father gets well again. They also talk about how they are going to let him know how much they love him and, most of all how, much he was missed.

"Why don't you children go to the park across the street and play while I talk with the doctor," Lynn says as she and the doctor walk back into the room. After the children are gone, the doctor continues to explain to Lynn and Howard how Willie's condition has worsened over the last few days. He lets them know that they might soon be asked if the oxygen system can be removed.

He also lets them know that Willie's insurance will soon be running out and that, when it does, he is going to sign the papers to have him removed from the hospital. He goes on to explain how "this hospital is a business, not a charity organization, and if they want charity, they should go and ask some of the northern agitators for it, while they are down here causing all this trouble."

Lynn takes a deep breath and looks the doctor right in the eyes . She shivers as the butterflies in her stomach flutter. Her voice trembles and cracks as the words come out, for she knows that a Black person's status in Mississippi is not one that allows them to speak harshly or course when talking to a White person period. Let alone one of prominence.

But, in a clear and direct voice, she says, "You keep my husband alive as long as you can! I don't care what it takes or what you need to do! You keep him alive! No matter what it takes, I will come up with your *damn* money!"

Howard doesn't say a word as he clenches both of his fists. It takes all that he has within to keep him from putting his hand on the doctor this day. For he knows well that this is Jim Crow's Mississippi. And the only thing putting his hands on the doctor would do is make things worst then they already are. So, he restrains himself.

The drive back to the house is a quiet one. Everybody just sits, looking out of the car windows and hardly saying a word. Once they have arrived back at Howard and Morgan's house, Lynn asks Howard not to discuss with the children what the doctor told them. They both agree that telling them would not help matters one bit.

After dinner, Lynn kisses the children goodnight and sends them off to bed early so that they will be well rested for school the next morning. Morgan gives Lynn an extra pillow for the couch, then they all bed down for the night.

As soon as Lynn nods off to sleep, her mind starts to drift. This dream involves a compelling male figure. In this dream, he and she are riding in a driverless carriage on a foggy road. As they both sit inside the carriage, the horse navigates the curves and turns of the path as if he knows exactly where he is going.

The stranger holds Lynn in his strong arms and kisses her lips ever so softly. He then whispers in her ear his desire to make love to her until the end of time as he slowly raises the ruffled, white, pink, and blue dress above her waist. As before, Lynn knows in her mind that this is wrong. But deep in her soul, she craves the stranger; she desires him as a young babe wants its mother's loving touch or a lover craves its soul mate after they've been separated for a long, long time.

With his strong arms extended out, the stranger pulls her underwear from her body and puts his face between her thighs. She digs her nails deep into the cushions of the carriage and gasps for air between her moans of ecstasy.

Once the carriage has come to a stop, the well-endowed being lifts her from the seat with his strong and sturdy arms and takes her over to a waiting blanket, where he gently sets her down.

While she neurotically waits, he slowly undresses, walks over to her, and placed his penis in her mouth. And without rumination, she starts to softly kiss on his organ. He then lies down next to her, and they suddenly seemingly become one.

"Lynn! Lynn! Wake up!" someone shouts. The shout is accompanied by several hard shakes. Lynn opens her eyes to find Morgan standing over her.

"Are you all right?" Morgan asks.

After taking a moment to clear her head, Lynn sits upright on the couch and replies, "I'm fine. Just having another one of those horrible dreams." As she pushes her hair back out of her face.

Morgan can see that she is soaking wet from sweat.

"I came out to check on you, and I saw that your eyes were open, but it seemed like you weren't breathing. That's when I started shaking you. Are you sure that you're all right? Because if you're not, I'll wake up Howard, and we can take you to the doctor. I know this sounds strange, but it was almost as if you had left your body."

"I'm sure I'm Ok," Lynn responds as she stands up.

"What kind of crazy dream were you having?" asks Morgan.

Lynn clears her throat and answers, "Oh, it's just a silly dream. It's probably from all the stuff that's going on. I'll be all right."

"You do know that we are here for you if you need us, don't you?" says Morgan as she gives Lynn a hug.

The next morning, after breakfast, Lynn, Howard, and Morgan sit in the living room, drinking coffee while the children clean up the breakfast dishes before heading out to school. Morgan stands up and asks, "Does anybody need any more coffee?"

Both Howard and Lynn answer, "Yes."

Morgan then picks up the empty cups and goes into the kitchen to refill them.

Howard looks at Lynn and says, "Morgan told me about what happened last night. And I know what's going on with Willie is weighing on you. Hell! It weighs on all of us. But is there anything else the matter? I noticed that something other than Willie might be bothering you. I saw it in your eyes when you first arrived. Now, what is it?"

Lynn answers while shaking her head, "It's a long story."

Howard replies, "We've got nothing but time, so tell me what's wrong."

Lynn first asks him if he remembers Madeline from the hospital.

He replies, "Vaguely."

She goes on to tell him about the similarities between what had happened to his brother, Willie, and what happened to Madeline's son, David. She tells him about all of the events that took place, including what they experienced in the cave. By the time she has finished, Howard is just sitting there in the chair with his mouth open.

After a moment of allowing what he has just heard to register, he responds, "Well...did you tell the police?"

Lynn answers, "Howard, you hardly believe me. Why in the world do you think they would? They would probably have me committed."

Howard shakes his head.

"I don't know what I'm going to do," she says.

Howard replies, "I wish I knew what to tell you."

Later that evening, after dinner, Lynn asks Howard if it would be ok if the children stayed with him and Morgan until the end of the school year—or at least until she can get to the bottom of what is going on. They agree that it would be best if they stayed there, but maybe Howard should return to Coffeeville with her.

After a lengthy discussion, Lynn finally convinces them that she has everything under control and that she will call him if things got out of hand. They both hug, and Lynn says her goodbyes to Morgan and the children before getting into the car to head back to Coffeeville.

Chapter 10

WRONG LOVE

THE HIGHWAY IS DARK, EXCEPT for the light emitted from the headlamps of the car, the stars in the sky, and the occasional wink of light from the distant farmhouses that peer through the tree line as the car speeds past. After driving for a while, she finds herself thinking about the old woman from her grandmother's story.

She wonders if she really has powers to heal. If so, could the woman still be alive today? And would she be of any help to her? *This is crazy,* she thinks. *There is no way in the world that woman could still be alive.*

As she continues to ponder the status of the old woman, she finds herself having to navigate a series of winding curves. As she comes around the last bend, the tree line suddenly opens, and she is met by a brilliantly lit object in the sky. This object is so large that it looks as if it has been painted onto a pitch-black, star-sprinkled canvas.

Its glow burns above the treetops like a giant beacon. And the thin line of soft clouds strung across its middle could not be more perfectly placed. It is the moon. And it is as if Lynn is just seeing it for the first time. It is full, and it sits just above the horizon.

At first look, it seems as if it is as big as the world itself. Which made it all the more spectacular.

The sight of something so magnificent and so vivid is both breathtaking and sobering to Lynn. The moment that she sees it, she knows that the possibility of things getting better is real. And for that moment, all her problems seem to have gone away. It is almost as if she can actually see Willie getting well, the children home, tucked securely in their beds asleep, and all of the things that she has endured over the last eleven and a half months being just a distant memory. Her entire world seems to be at peace.

Once back home, Lynn gets undressed and puts on her housecoat. She fills the bathtub and turns on the radio. It is tuned to her and Willie's favorite station. She reminisces about how she and Willie would dance while listening to it for seemingly hours at a time.

As she listens and hums along with the soothing music, she builds a fire in the fireplace and lights the stove to heat the kettle. Before long, steam starts to rise from the pot as the water begins to boil. Lynn retrieves a small bucket from the kitchen cabinet and dips water from the kettle.

She swirls her fingers around in the in the tub to check the temperature as she pours the hot water from the bucket into the bathtub. After setting the empty bucket on the mantle, she removes her robe and lowers her tired body down into the warm water. As the warm water soothes her tense muscles, she continues to sing along with the radio.

After a while, the singing turns to humming and then into light snoring as she nods off to sleep.

While she sleeps, her mind once again takes her to a place that she is not familiar with. This place is dimly lit and warm. It has a soft, continuous breeze blowing, and several hot springs are feeding several steaming pools of water.

In this dream, Lynn sees herself dressed in a black satin nightgown, lying by one of the pools of water, patiently waiting for someone. As the steam from the warm water moistens her soft brown skin, she hums a melody, slowly swirling her fingers around in the water.

Then, seemingly out of nowhere, the silhouette of a man appears off in the distance. From the shape of the profile, she can tell that he is tall with a lean, muscular body. And as this muscular figure makes its way across the shallow pools of water toward her, she sees herself smiling as if she and he are very familiar with each other.

Once he has emerged out of the mist, she sees that he has only a towel wrapped around the lower half of his body. She watches herself in the dream beckon for the stranger to come closer. She strains as she tries to make out the man's face, for he seems almost faceless.

He pauses only for a moment to greet her before stepping into the pool. As he slowly wades across to her, she lowers herself down into the water. Once they are face to face, they embrace with open arms.

He slowly removes the satin from her wet body and lifts her up and sits her on the side of the pool. He then kisses her lips as she wraps both her legs around his waist. And as the towel floats away, she tries with all her might to awaken from the erotic dream, for she knows in her heart that she loves and belongs to Willie and only Willie. But she finds herself not only unable to resist but very actively receptive and a willing participant throughout the entire romantic encounter.

Early the next morning, Lynn is awakened by the ringing of the telephone. She finds herself lying on the bathroom floor, nude, with no recollection of how she got there. She feels as if she hasn't slept a wink all night. As she slowly gets to her feet, the phone rings again and again.

After wrapping a towel around her naked body, she walks into the front room and picks up the receiver. And in a low, raspy voice, she says, "Hello?"

The person on the other end then replies, "Hello, Lynn. It's me, Howard. I've been trying to get in touch with you all night!"

"There is nothing wrong with the kids, is there?" Lynn asks.

Howard quickly answers, "No, it's not the kids. They're fine. It's about Willie."

"What about Willie?" she asks.

After a moment of silence, Howard answers, "He has gotten a lot worse. It started yesterday shortly after you left."

Lynn slowly sinks down to the floor as the tears start rolling down her cheeks. Howard tries to comfort her, but he, too, is soon overwhelmed with emotion and starts to cry as well. After a while, Lynn composes herself and asks Howard if the children know.

Howard answers, "No, I thought it would be best if you told them."

She asks Howard to bring the children to the phone one at a time, starting with the oldest. As she explains to them what has happened to their father, she tells them that, with a little faith everything will work itself out. She also tells them that they mean the world to him and that he would want them to be strong. And although things are not looking good right now, he will continue to try and get better.

She assures them that she loves them more than life itself and that she will do everything in her power to continue to protect them. After she has finished, she asks them to put their uncle back on the phone.

"Howard," she says. "You know that your brother is my whole world, and I don't know what I'm going to do if he doesn't make it. I need for you to try and keep my children calm until I make it back down there. I will be leaving out as soon as I can."

After hanging up the phone, she goes into her bedroom, lies across the bed, and starts to cry once again. This time, she cries not for Willie but about the dream that she had. It was a dream that seemed all too real, and she feels as if she was unfaithful to him.

Although in her mind, she knows that it was just a dream, her body is telling her that it was so much more. Her body is telling her that it was real in every sense of the word and that, in some strange way, she wanted it to be.

After she's lain there for twenty minutes or so, the phone rings again. She takes a moment to get herself together before she gets up to answer it. It is Madeline, and right away, Madeline can tell that something is terribly wrong.

"What's wrong?" she asks.

Lynn clears her throat and tells her that Howard called and said that Willie has gotten worse. Madeline attempts to comfort Lynn, but she soon becomes overwhelmed with grief and starts to cry, for she knows all too well that her beloved son, David, could quickly suffer the same fate as Willie.

The two ladies try to cheer each other up by talking about the good times that they shared with Willie and David and how they wish they had met under better circumstances. Madeline asks Lynn if it would be ok if she rides with her when she returns to Jackson.

Lynn replies, "I would love to have the company, but I need to make a little detour, if it's ok with you."

Madeline responds, "I'm riding with you."

They both agree that they will leave at 3:00 p.m. so that they will have enough time to do what Lynn needs to do and still get to Jackson before it gets too late.

Chapter 11

A SECRET

As soon as Lynn turns onto Madeline's street, she checks the address that Madeline wrote down, and she immediately notices the large upscale houses and the sidewalks that extend from one end of the block to the other. *This has got to be the wrong address*, she thinks as she drives past the neighboring houses with their well-trimmed lawns and neatly cut hedges and bushes. To her, they look as if they were done by a manicurist rather than by the two Black men working in the front yard of one of the houses. A couple of the yards even have fountains and statues of naked angels in them.

Once she arrives at the address written on the paper, she hesitantly parks her car in the driveway and walks up and rings the doorbell. Madeline opens the door almost immediately and greets her with a sympathetic smile. The two ladies hug, and Madeline invites her in.

"I have a few more things that I need to pack, and I will be ready," Madeline says as she walks back into the bedroom. The two of them try hard not to make direct eye contact, for they know that, if they do, they will break down and start crying all over again.

"I called the hospital yesterday," Madeline says as she walks into the other room to finish packing. "I'm having David moved to another hospital. I think his doctor has a problem having him for a patient, if you know what I mean."

"I do know what you mean, and I would like to do the same for Willie once I get this insurance thing worked out," Lynn replies.

Lynn walks around and looks at the numerous pictures that Madeline has on her walls and in a large oak-and-glass curial cabinet. In one of the pictures, there is a younger Madeline, her two sons, and a man. The man has one arm around Madeline and the other around the boys. One of the things most noticeable in the pictures background was the Golden Gate Bridge with its glowing cables and steel structure.

"Who is this guy in the picture with you and the boys?" Lynn asks in a voice loud enough for Madeline to hear in the other room.

"That's their dad. He and I divorced six years ago," Madeline answers as she walks back into the room, carrying a small suitcase.

"It was a very ugly divorce, to say the least," she goes on to say.

"How long were you guys married?" Lynn asks.

"Twenty-two years. And that was about twenty-one years too long. Looking back, I truly believe that that man cheated on me from day one and continued on cheating until the day our divorce was final," she answers with a chuckle.

"The day that David got hired at that gas station, I had him helping me clean out the attic. That was when we found a box of his dad's things. Among the things in the box was a bundle of letters from one of his old lovers. I guess he must have forgotten that he had hidden them up there when he moved out.

"You see, neither one of the boys ever knew the real reason why their father and I parted company, until that moment. Their father was someone that they both worshiped and wanted to be like. Which was a good thing, being that he was one of the few Negro attorneys ever hired by the railroad. And I guess I just didn't have the heart to change what he was in their eyes. So, I never told them.

"He started reading them before I knew what it was that he had found. By the time I noticed that he was reading something and realized what it was, it was too late. I asked him not to read them. But you know how stubborn young men can sometimes be. And he just wasn't going to take no for an answer. The more he read, the angrier he became."

"And his father is no longer alive. He died in a car accident; it will be three years, come this July. So, he turned his anger toward me. I guess, maybe I should have told them sooner? Who knows?" she concludes as she puts on her coat and walks toward the door.

"So where is this detour?" Madeline asks.

"It is to see if someone is still alive," Lynn replies.

"To see if someone's still alive?" Madeline repeats.

Lynn then tells her the story that her grandmother told her and what her grandmother said she had witnessed. *If that old woman's still alive, that will make her about a hundred and fifty years old*, Madeline thinks. But knowing the stress that Lynn is under, Madeline keeps the thought to herself.

Sensing Madeline's nonverbal questioning of her state of mind, Lynn blurts, "I know it's a long shot!"

"Yes! A very long shot," Madeline replies in a shallow but sarcastic voice.

As they enter the town of Charleston, Lynn starts to recall her teenage years. She remembered things like when she and Willie first started dating and how they would sometimes sneak out at night and meet up town. And how they would meet out behind his parents' barn and make out until the wee hours of the night.

She recalls that it was the Friday and Saturday evenings that they both loved so much. That was because those where the evenings Willie played baseball. And baseball was king in the Delta. Willie was one of the stars on the Charleston's Negro team, and boy, could he steal bases. There was one game in which he stole five bases. That was a team record that stood for years.

She remembers when a lot of the Black communities in the Delta had their own unofficial ball teams. When these teams played baseball against one another, the people on the field and in the stands were able to temporally remove themselves from some of their worst woes. It allowed them to escape the sometimes seemingly constant grind that the system of Jim Crow had put upon them.

The ballgames were the well-needed escape and were usually the pinnacle of what was a long, hard, and sometimes dehumanizing week for most of those that lived in the Delta at that time. And no matter who won, there was always the promise of "Our team will win next time."

She recalls how she and her cousin would sit in the stands and cheer as their team racked up the points. And how after each and every game, Willie would act as if the fact that their team won was no big deal to him. It was as if Willie somehow knew and understood that, no matter who won the game, shortly after it was over, the reality of life there would remain the same.

As they drive through the center of town, visions of how things were in the not-so-distant past flows through her mind. Back when she and Willie were too young to get inside of the blues joints—so they sat outside, held hands, and just listened to the music as the musicians played inside. That was back when Willie first told her that he loved her. And at that moment, they both knew, way back then, that it would last forever.

Not too long after leaving the center of the town, they come to a small bridge. Once across, the paved surface becomes a gravel road that leads down between two plowed-over cotton fields. As the car travels down the road, the dust from the gravel rises high into the air. Off in the distance, they can see a row of sharecropper shacks set off to one side of the road. As they get closer to the shacks, they see people standing on the front porch of one of the tiny structures.

As Lynn slows down, a tall Black man wearing overalls and a straw hat, accompanied by a little boy—which looks to be around eight or maybe nine years old—walks out onto the road. The little boy is slim with a dark complexion, and he is dressed in an old pair of pants that come up just past his ankles, with no shirt or shoes on. He has big pretty brown eyes, and his hair is short and needs trimming. The boy stands next to the bearded man as Madeline watches in silence. He shivers as the crisp autumn air surrounds his sparsely clothed body.

The man is also dark in complexion with a rough-looking, thin beard, and he has a large chew of tobacco tucked behind his lower lip . Madeline rolls down the window and greets them with a friendly hello as they walk up to the car. The man tips his hat as he returns the friendly greeting. Lynn explains to the gentleman that they are looking for a house near the creek where an old woman—or possibly her relatives—might live. She says it is rumored that the old woman is older than the creek itself and has a lot of cats.

The more Lynn talks, the bigger the man's eyes get. He then clears his throat and spits some tobacco juice onto the ground.

"Why you all looking for Ms. Irma?" the man asks as he wipes the cuff of his flannel shirt across his mouth.

"We have some business with her," Lynn explains.

The man takes the little boy by the hand, "That old woman's nothing but trouble, you hear me?" He then spits on the ground once more. "You best steer clear of her if you know what's good for you!" he shouts as he and the young boy turn and walk back toward the shack. Once they are back at the shack, the man goes inside and slams the door shut, leaving the little boy on the porch.

As Lynn and Madeline start to drive off, the little boy comes running back up to the car. Madeline rolls down the window and asks the boy, "And what can I do for you, my handsome young man?"

The boy replies with a smile, "Five cents, and I'll show you where the old lady lives." Madeline smiles back and says, "Here's a dollar. Get in."

As they drive on, the gravel road soon becomes a dirt road with lots of potholes in it. After a while, they come to a fork.

"She lives straight down that road. You can't miss it," says the little boy. "And this is where I get out. Good luck!" He gets out of the car. He then takes off running back toward the shack.

Chapter 12

MS. IRMA

"THAT MUST BE THE HOUSE there," Madeline says as they come upon the only house that they have seen since they passed the row of sharecropper's shacks. The house sits on large cinderblocks and has a screened-in front porch with an old chicken coup, which can be seen from the road, sitting in the back yard.

Near the chicken coup sits an old single shear plow. The plow is used as a centerpiece for one of the most beautiful flower gardens that Lynn and Madeline have ever seen. The entire area around the house is just saturated with flower beds and hanging potted plants.

As Lynn and Madeline get out of the car and walk toward the house, they see hummingbirds retrieving nectar from the flowers planted in the two large boiling pots that sit on both sides of the entrance to the screened-in porch. Madeline looks around in amazement as Lynn asks her in a voice of disbelief, "Did you notice something strange about this place?"

Madeline replies, "Yes! It's beautiful."

Lynn responds, "No! It's autumn, and the flowers are still alive."

Lynn knocks on the porch door several times, and no one answers. They then walk around to the back of the house to check and see if anyone is home. As they come around the side of the house, they see a heavy-set woman sitting in a fan-back wicker chair next to a table under a rather large pecan tree. The woman has a bright blue knitted shawl wrapped around her upper body and a head full of long silver-gray hair.

Lynn waves and shouts hello as they walk down a slightly sloping hill toward the woman. The woman doesn't acknowledge their presence. She just sits motionlessly in the chair as if she is deaf or severely hard of hearing.

Once they are within a few feet of her, she slowly looks up at them. Displaying little or no facial expression, she looks back down at the cat in her lap. This leads Lynn and Madeline to think that, in some strange way, she has been expecting them. She takes Lynn by the hand and squeezes it tight. While clutching Lynn's hand, she gazes cavernously into her eyes and mumbles something under her breath. Madeline is somewhat terrified, yet she looks on in astonishment.

The old woman speaks. "How long have you been having the dreams?"

At first, Lynn starts to lie, for she is ashamed to tell anyone or even admit to having such erotic delusions. Lynn feels that the dreams make her, in some strange way, adulterous toward Willie.

"What dreams?" Lynn replies.

The old lady then says, "To others, you may lie, but to your heart, lying is not an option." Lynn exhales and says, "For about a week now."

As the old woman continues to stare into Lynn's eyes, she asks, "Have you succumbed to them yet?"

"What do you mean by succumbed to them yet?" asks Lynn. "It's only a dream."

"It only seems like a dream," Ms. Irma explains. "But there will come a time when what is seemingly a dream will become a reality."

Lynn snatches her hand away from the old woman.

As Ms. Irma rises up from the chair and starts to walk toward the house, she looks back over her shoulder at Madeline and asks, "Are you also having the dreams?"

Madeline quickly responds in a nervous stuttering voice, "Yes, yes I am. But they are not erotic in nature. They are more frightening than anything else."

"Good," says the old woman, nodding her head. She then continues her slow walk toward the house, with Lynn and Madeline following close behind.

Once inside the house, she asks Lynn and Madeline to have a seat while she stirs up the ashes in the potbelly stove with the poker. She then sits down in a rocking chair that is covered with several folded patched quilt for padding.

As soon as she sits down, several cats come running to her side. While the cats curl themselves around her legs, she pulls a snuff can from her pocket and puts a pinch in her mouth. She then picks up one of the cats and places it in her lap and starts to rub its head and back as Madeline and Lynn start to tell her about the events that took place. They even tell her about Willie, David, and what happened when they went to the gas station.

After they have finished, Ms. Irma asks, "So, what is it that you women want from me?" Lynn looks over at Madeline and then back at the woman and clears her throat.

She utters, "We need your help. That is, we need to know if you can help us or will help us."

"Why should I involve myself in matters that are not of my concern?" asks Ms. Irma.

"A person once told me a story. The story was about a woman that had done a huge favor for someone that she had never met before. This deed was done not because of the love the woman carried in her heart but for the love that the stranger carried in his for someone else," Lynn explains.

Lynn then goes on to tell the woman about what her grandmother witnessed and that she was the only one her grandmother had ever told that story to.

"How do you know that I am the woman in the story?" asks Ms. Irma as the big yellow cat jumps down out of her lap and walks over to Lynn. The cat starts to rub its body against her leg.

"I don't know," Lynn replies as she bends down, picks up the cat, and places it on her lap. The cat purrs as Lynn rubs its back.

"I see that Mama cat likes you," Ms. Irma says as she opens the door of the potbelly stove and spits the juices from the snuff onto the bright yellow and red flames.

"Not saying that I am who you think I am, but if I am and if I was to help you, what will you two ladies be willing to give me in return?" Ms. Irma asks.

"How much money would it take?" asks Madeline as she opens her purse to retrieve her checkbook.

The old woman chuckles slightly as she answers, "Money? Money and things of monetary value are only valuable to the beings of this world. I am afraid that this is one of those things that can't be obtained by the mere exchange of legal tender. This is something that will require more of a—should I say—spiritual compensation."

"What do you mean by spiritual compensation?" asks Lynn.

"First, I think that I should tell you ladies about what you are dealing with," says Ms. Irma. "When a land has been burdened with the weight of deep and deliberate unholy afflictions of the human flesh for so many years, like this here Delta has, the beings from the between world of life and death, find this place desirable…should I say? And the untimely releasing of all those souls directly affects the actions taken on the living. Be it sanctioned by religion, color of skin, or social status."

She then continues on to say, "This thing that you described to me sounds like a type of devil or demon of the worst kind. I felt its aura all about you the moment you stepped out of your car. This type of fowl spirit is more commonly referred to as a lamia, succubus, or succubae of a sort.

"Throughout time, there have been many stories about these creatures. Some of the tales are about things that were good and beautiful. But most were not." The old woman stands up, walks over to the window, and adjusts the curtains to block the direct rays of the sun from entering the room. She then walks over to the potbelly stove and closes the door and sits back down.

"Some were about how lamias would entice unsuspecting individuals into entering a bedroom, dark forest, or sometimes even graveyards by preying on two of the humans' most sensitive feelings. Desire and sympathy. They disguised themselves as beautiful women or men—or even a child—willing to please in any way that they could. Or maybe someone that's been hurt in some way and requires help. Once the victims entered into the trap, they were in most cases, never seen or heard from again.

"And others were about how a succubus would enchant the body of a corps and masquerade as a would-be lover or a person of the evening so that it could nibble away at the soul of some love-struck fool or would-be costumer. Whichever the case may have been at the time," Ms. Irma explains.

As she continues to talk, Lynn and Madeline both sit quietly and listen to her every word. "They all have one thing in common, and that is that they are all merchants of souls." "What do you mean when you say merchants of souls?" Madeline asks.

"What I mean is that they can only exist as long as those they trick into having ill-begotten feelings for them, continue to express their feelings with earthly gifts. Or when someone passes something on to them that has caused their heart great pain—and the item was given unto them with evil or malicious intent. When this item is passed on to the demon, it will cause the originator great grief and displeasure for the remainder of their time with the living and, sometimes, even after death. Unless the item is retrieved."

"From what you ladies have told me, it seems that you do have one thing in your favor. Your men haven't given up yet. But when and if they do, they will…die! And after their death, the demon will probably retrieve their corps, and they will walk among the living once more. But this time, as slaves of the demon. The thing to understand about this kind of creature is that it feeds on evil like the bees feed on the nectar from the flowers in my garden or a newborn babe on the breast of its mother. It is the sole purpose of their existence."

After the woman has finished, Lynn and Madeline sit motionlessly, gazing at the flames contained within the rustic stove.

After several long minutes, Lynn breaks the silence. "Is there any way that one could free themselves or their loved ones from the curse without retrieving the item?" she asks.

"No! That item is what connects their souls to the creature. And it must be retrieved first so that the link can be broken," answers the old woman. "These demons always keep these items in or around their haunt. And they are often held in bottles or jars. Their haunts are usually located in very dark places, like caves or tunnels. Because in the light of day, they are frail, weak, and can spew no evil or conceal their true selves.

"If you decide to enter a demon's lair, you best be watchful of their slaves." She then adds, "There are several things that you will need to remember. The first is that these demons can only walk the earth in a human form during the autumn. That is from the first new moon after the start of the season until the winter solstice, which is the shortest day of the year. After that, they only exist in spirit form until the next season. Another thing is that they try to avoid the daylight as much as possible. Because in the daylight, you see them not as they want you to see them, but as they truly are.

"And the last thing is that they are territorial, meaning that they will always keep their lair within a four or five-mile radius of where it was the year before—for their entire existence, if possible."

Lynn moves as if she is about to ask the old woman another question, but the woman interrupts her before she can get it out of her mouth. "I have told you more than I should have without discussing my compensation," says the old woman.

"What would you have us do in return for your help?" asks Madeline.

Without hesitation, the old woman answers, "You must revisit the lair and retrieve all of the containers. And being that you don't know which of the items belong to your loved ones, you must bring them all to me, and I will separate them out. Remember! Once you have all of the containers in your possession, don't tarry!

"For as soon as the demons find out what you have done, all hell will break loose. And I do mean that, in a real sense."

The old woman then looks over at Lynn and says, "I will do what is needed to free their souls, but the remaining items I will keep as payment for my deed."

Chapter 13

THE REALITY

Driving back down the gravel road , they see the little boy once more. He is sitting out in front of the old shack on a wooden create just off to the side of the road. His face lights up with a big smile as he sees the car entering the clearing. It looks as if he has been waiting for a while and is delighted to see that the old woman hasn't devoured them or changed them into some inanimate object.

He waves both hands in the air and runs behind the car as it drives past. Lynn waves back at him and watches him through the rearview mirror until the dust from the gravel road obstructs the view. She then looks over at Lynn and smiles.

As they make their way toward the main roadway to Jackson, they talk about the things that the old woman discussed with them, and they try to figure out if they have any other options. Lynn and Madeline even briefly consider going to the newspaper with the story. But they both understand the complexities of being people of color in the

Delta; most likely, their story would land them in a mental institution .

As they pull onto the main highway, they are almost run off the road by a speeding police car that seemingly comes out of nowhere. As the vehicle passes, it turns on its siren and flashing lights. The officer on the passenger side sticks his head out of the window and yells out a vulgar racial insult and give them a menacing stare. Lynn grips the steering wheel with both hands as she struggles to maintain control.

After finally bringing the car to a stop on the shoulder of the highway, she looks over at Madeline and asks if she is ok.

Madeline nods her head and says, "Yes," and she exhales a breath of relief. She then screams out, "Out of all the things that we have been through, we still have to put up with this Jim Crow bullshit!"

Lynn slowly nods her head in agreement. Soon after pulling back onto the road, they come across the same officer who nearly caused them to crash. He and his partner have a car with four young men in it pulled over to the side of the road. Lynn and Madeline can see that one of the men is White and the other three are Black. They also notice that the car has New Jersey license plates.

Lynn looks straight ahead as she slows down, but she continues to move forward. Madeline watches as the officers pull one of the men from the car and push him to the ground while yelling at him. As they slowly drive past, she sees one of the officers hit one of the men in the groin with his nightstick while the second officer watches and laughs.

They then start to pull the third man from the car, but they stop when the one officer, who happens to have a large torso, looks up and sees that Madeline is watching them physically assault the young men. He marches toward their car while motioning for them to hurry up and move on. As they drive past, Lynn continues to look forward at the road in front of them—without showing any expressions. Madeline looks him in the face while he yells racist insults at them.

The reflections of the patrol car flashing lights shrink until they disappear in the rearview mirror. But the images of the incident, is forever engraved in their memory. They both feel that they need a moment to reflect and maybe digest what just happened.

After a while, Lynn tries to start a conversating about the kids. But it was inevitable that once they started to talk, the conversation would gravitate to things like racism, bigotry, and how Jim Crow has made the south so unbearable for people of color, that some are willing to leave everything that they and their families has worked their whole lives for and move to the north.

Chapter 14

A VISITOR IN THE NIGHT

It IS LATE WHEN THEY get to Jackson, so Lynn drops Madeline off at her hotel and starts heading toward Howard's house. After thinking about it for a moment, she changes her mind and goes to the hospital instead. Once at the hospital, she takes the stairs to the floor that Willie's ward is on.

As she steps out of the stairwell and into the hallway, she doesn't see anyone at the nurse's station. But she does hear giggling coming from behind it. So she walks up to the counter and looks over it. She sees a partly disrobed nurse on the floor with a partially undressed orderly.

They both hastily scramble to their feet while adjusting their clothes. The orderly looks at Lynn with a sheepish smile on his face as he quickly walks off down the hall. The nurse, after straightening her clothes, attempts to act as if nothing was happening.

She asks Lynn, "And what can I do for you?"

Lynn, not wanting to make an uncomfortable situation even more uncomfortable for either of them, simply asks, "How is my husband, Willie, doing tonight?"

The two ladies talk briefly about Willie's condition. During the conversation, the nurse tells her that she needs to speak with his doctor if she wants more detailed information about how he is doing.

The nurse also explains to her that the doctor won't be in until around 10:00 a.m. tomorrow morning. And if she wants to, she can spend the night. Lynn thanks the nurse and then walks into the ward where Willie is kept. After entering the ward, she walks over to Willie's bed and sits down in the chair next to it.

Before long, Lynn finds herself sitting and staring at Willie's motionless body as she reminisces about their past. She holds his hand and rubs his face and forehead as she weeps from time to time. As the night grows late, the events of the day and the long drive begin to take their toll on her, and she drifts off to sleep.

This night rest is the best night rest that Lynn has had in a long time. For it is not accompanied by the complicated yet alluring dreams that routinely come with the closing of her eyes. It is a night of pure peace and undisturbed rest, until around 4:00 a.m. At that time, she is awakened by a squeaky noise.

As she slowly opens her eyes, she sees a shadow moving about the room. Her heart throbs as she thinks about the wicked creature. It must have crept in to finish off both her and her helpless husband. She keeps very still as she watches the figure move about the ward.

The shadowy character navigates its way around the obstacles in the dark ward as if it has not only been in the ward on several occasions but placed each and every bed and chair in its place. After making its way over to the row of closets containing the patients' belongings, it patiently and meticulously goes through them one by one. Taking anything that it can find of value. With its arms full, it then heads toward the nightstand next to Willie's bed.

But before it can make it to the nightstand, it drops some of its stolen goods and bends down to retrieve them. Several coins fall from its top pocket. As the coins hit the floor, they bounce and roll in all directions, breaking the uneasy stillness of the room.

The figure freezes in its tracks until the noises of the coins striking and rolling about the floor fade away. Silence reenters the room—except for the sound of a single rolling coin . As this single coin starts its journey, Lynn can see the would-be thief following the sound it produces as it rolled across the room, stopping only after running into her foot.

As the sound from the rolling coin ends, so does the movement of the figure's head as it fixes on Lynn's silhouette. Slowly, the figure rises from its kneeling position. Lynn closes her eyes and pretends that she is asleep as it studies her body from across the room. With the room being as dark as it is, the not-so-cunning intruder assumes that Lynn's asleep and hastily exits the ward.

Lynn realizes that it wasn't the hideous creature at all but just some thief taking advantage of poor sick people's misfortunes. She gets up and walks over to the door and peeks through the glass into the well-lighted hallway. She sees the characterless individual as he makes his way down the hall and into the next ward. Lynn looks over at the nurse's desk and sees that there is no one staffing it. She then props a chair up against the door, and returns to the chair next to Willie's bed and sits back down.

Early the next morning, she is awakened by the noise of someone trying to force their way into the room. At first, it startles her as thoughts of the scoundrel returning rapidly rush into her mind. But as her eyes open and focus, she can see that it is the night-shift nurse, so she hurries over and removes the chair from the front of the door.

"Why in the heck did you put a chair in front of the door?" asks the nurse.

"I was sitting there, using the light from the hall to read and forgot to move it after I was done. Sorry about that," Lynn replies.

"I just wanted to wake you before the doctors get in. They might have a problem if they knew I allowed you to spend the night. They see that privilege as being reserved for only...well, you know what I mean."

"Yes, I do know what you mean. And I want to thank you for allowing me to do so. I have not rested this sound since God knows when," Lynn says as she stands up and stretches. She then asks the nurse if she can use the phone at the front desk to call a relative and let him know that she is in town.

After using the phone, she returns to the room and watches as the nurse takes Willie's vitals .

"Umm...that's strange. This guy barely had a pulse yesterday, and now it's almost normal. Let me recheck his charts. I'll be right back," the nurse says as she leaves the room.

Lynn kneels down next to Willie's bed, kisses his lips, and whispers, "Just keep on trying, baby. Together we can beat this."

After whispering a short prayer for Willie and the kids, she walks out to the waiting room to wait for the doctor to show up.

Chapter 15

A WALK IN THE PARK

AFTER AN HOUR OR SO, the doctor finally shows up.

"Good morning," Lynn says as she attempts to be as cordial as her true feelings about the man will allow her to be.

"Yea. Uh huh. Good morning," he grunts in his usual condescending manner. After viewing Willie's chart for only a few seconds, he looks up at Lynn and starts to speak.

But before he can get a word out, Lynn cuts him off.

"The nurse said that his vital signs are looking a lot better today. That's a good thing, isn't it?"

He turns his head in her direction but never makes eye contact and says, "As I was about to say! His vitals have improved a little over the night, but it's probably something temporary. If not, we will let you know."

He turns and starts to walk away, but then he suddenly stops and turns back around after only taking a few steps. "Oh yes, there is one more thing. You will need to see the people down in billing and make some arrangements for payment before you leave today. It looks like your insurance has just about run out...Have a good day."

Just as the doctor walks off, Howard walks up.

"Good morning!" he says, reaching out to give Lynn a hug .

"What did you do? Drive here in the middle of the night?" he asks.

"No. Actually, Madeline and I drove down late yesterday. After dropping her at her hotel, I came straight here, and the good nurse allowed me to spend the night in the chair next to Willie's bed."

"Ok, so how is he doing?" Howard asks while nodding his head.

"The doctor is downplaying it, but he is actually doing a little bit better, I think," Lynn answers. She then goes on to tell Howard first about the nurse and orderly making out and then about the thief.

"I've heard about him. Rumor has it that he has impregnated several of the mental patients in the female ward and that the hospital is protecting its reputation by giving the women abortions and denying that a problem even exists."

"So, did you see what he looks like?" Howard asks.

"No, not really," Lynn answers.

"The doctors and the people running this hospital are very well connected and could cause a lot of problems for someone. Especially if they thought that someone could cause problems for them or this place. I personally wouldn't get involved with this unless someone puts their hand on Willie, if I were you.

"And another thing. I wouldn't leave anything of value here that belongs to Willie anyway. There is nothing of any importance for them to take. Nope! I wouldn't open my mouth about this for all the tea in China. Besides that, it's the White folk business. And we colored folks always come up short when we get in the middle of White folk business. You've been around Lynn, and you know it as well as I do," Howard continues on to say.

With some reluctance, Lynn eventually agrees with him. "I know you just got here, but there are a few things that we need to talk about, but right now, I really need to get downstairs to billing before they get crowded. Because if I don't get there before the crowd does, I will be there all morning. You can wait if you like, or I'll meet you back at the house before you go to work this evening." Lynn then picks up her purse and heads toward the elevator.

It is still early, so she is the first to arrive at the window. And it doesn't take long for them to tell her pretty much what she already knows: that the money is about to run out and that Willie will have to be sent to a state facility when it does.

Lynn still doesn't want to face what is quickly becoming a truth. And part of that truth is that Willie just isn't going to get any better and that she and the children will now and forever have to face life alone. And the other sad part of that truth is that she has no ideas about how they are going to do it.

Before going back to Willie's ward, she decides to take a walk through the park, which is across the street from the hospital. She feels that the walk might calm her and give her some time to pull herself back together before talking to Howard. After walking for a while, she takes a seat on a bench that is facing the hospital.

As she looks out at the skyline, she can't help but notice how huge and sprawling the hospital is. It looks as if the facility stretches on for blocks. And each and every bush and tree has been put in place with a lot of consideration for the overall view. This living portrait has but one obstruction from where she is sitting, and that is a rather large weeping willow, which sits unaccompanied on a grassy knoll in front of the park .

The branches on the tree stretch out from its trunk as if it is trying to block out the entire sky, but then they gradually turn downward, creating a draping yet somber appearance. The longer she looks at the massive tree, the eerier it becomes. And as her goosebumps start to rise, she decides that it is best that she heads back.

While walking back to the hospital, she decides to stop and take a closer look at the awesome-looking willow tree. She stops at the edge of the knoll, which is about fifty feet away from the outer edges of its massive outreaching branches. She can't help but notice the parade of honeybees going to and from this magnificent creation of Mother Nature's. After venturing closer and peeking through the draping canopy, she sees the large opening that starts at the base of the tree and extends upward about six feet. This is where the bees are going to and coming from.

Lynn slowly sticks her head into the opening and looks up and sees the largest beehive she has ever seen in her entire life. The hive is covered with thousands of bees, and there are literally dozens of them coming and going at any given moment. After seeing all of the bees, Lynn slowly eases away from the tree and walks back to the hospital.

After returning to the hospital, she and Howard sit and visit with Willie as they try to come up with what their options are going to be once the insurance runs out. After a long and serious conversation, they realize that they only have two choices. One is to let him go to the state hospital, and the other is to take him home.

Knowing that sending him off to the state-run hospital would be sending him off to die, they decide that it would be best to just take him home.

Chapter 16

NO GOOD OPTIONS

"Good morning," Morgan says as she opens the curtains in the living room.

With her eyes scrunched from the sunlight, Lynn replies, "Good morning! What time is it?"

"It's almost noon. Did you sleep well?" Morgan asks.

"Not really. Still having them damn dreams," she answers as she sits upright on the couch and puts her feet on the floor. Morgan sets a cup of coffee down on the table in front of her. "Drink this. It might make you feel better."

Morgan sits down on the couch next to her and asks, "Have you ever considered going to see a doctor about these dreams? Maybe he'll give you something to help you sleep."

"Yes, but I think he might ask too many questions, and I'll end up in a mental institution instead." Morgan chuckles as Lynn takes a sip of the coffee. "I told the kids not to wake you because I thought you needed your rest. You looked really beat yesterday, so Howard took them to the store with him. They should be back in about an hour or so."

Lynn replies with a thank you as she stands, stretches, and heads to the bathroom.

Once Howard and the kids return from the store, everybody eats lunch and then heads back to the hospital to visit with Willie. After being at the hospital for only a short while, the nurse comes into the room and tells them that they have to leave because it is time to clean Willie up and feed him.

After the kids walk out of the room, the nurse explains to Lynn and Howard that they can stay on if they want to, but his feeding through a feeding tube might be a little upsetting for the children to watch. Or, if they wanted, they could come back later because, after feeding him, they are going to set him up in his chair by the window so that he can get some sun and look out at the park while his food digests. Lynn thanks the nurse once more for allowing her to spend the night and for taking such good care of Willie.

Later that evening after, talking with Madeline, Lynn decided it is time they headed back. So, after saying her goodbyes to the family, she goes and picks up Madeline and heads toward the highway home.

"I think we'd best stop here for gas before getting on the highway," Madeline says after seeing a gas station just ahead at the next corner. "And I do believe this next fill-up is on me, being that we are in your car. And I won't take no for an answer." She pulls her wallet from her purse.

As Lynn pulls the car up to the gas pump, a bell rings, and a teenage boy walks out of the office and over to the car.

"Fill her up?" he asks.

"Yes, if you would please, and check the oil," Lynn answers.

"It's late, and you look tired." Madeline says. "I think I need to drive, and I'm not going to take no for an answer about that either. And besides, you drove all the way here, and we both know that you have a lot on your mind". Madeline motions for Lynn to get out from behind the wheel so she can scoot over.

Lynn nods her head and gets out of the car and stretches while Madeline scoots across the seat. Once the car is filled with gas, Madeline pays the boy, and the ladies head for the main highway. By the time they make it to the main road, Lynn is fast asleep.

While sleeping, her mind takes her to another place that she is not familiar with. She finds herself alone in a wooded area. Yet off in the far distance, she can see a large meadow with a solitary tree positioned in the middle of it. In this dream, she is dressed in a bright yellow-flowered dress and is sitting on a large patched quilt.

In the distance , she sees a man riding a large black horse heading in her direction. As he gets closer, she can see the silhouette of his muscular body. She then knows that it is the same stranger that visited her in the other dreams. Lynn tries hard to awaken from this dream. But it seems as if her body and her soul refuse to let her.

As the tall stranger gets down off of the horse, Lynn tries with all her might to make out his face, but it is as if he has a face and, at the same time, is faceless. The stranger lowers himself down on to the quilt beside her warm body and starts to cuddle her in his strong arms. The closer he pulls her to him, the more she wants to be there. He gently begins to unbutton her bright yellow dress with his strong hands.

"Wake up! Wake up! You are having a nightmare," says Madeline while shaking Lynn. Lynn opens her eyes and realizes that she is no longer in the woods with the stranger but still in the car with Madeline.

"How long have I been asleep?" she asks.

"A little bit over an hour or so," Madeline answers.

"Pull over. I need to stretch my legs a little bit," says Lynn.

Madeline pulls the car over onto the shoulder of the road, and Lynn gets out and walks around. She then tells Madeline to scoot over. "I'll take it from here." But as soon as Lynn gets behind the wheel, a police car pulls off the road behind them and turns on its bright-red flashing lights. The two ladies look at each other in confusion because they know that they haven't committed any crime.

As soon as the officer walks up to the car, both ladies immediately recognize him from the incident with the four young men. They can tell that he doesn't remember them from the way he starts the conversation: "You all must not be from around here, are you?" he asks with a deliberate touch of sarcasm as he bends down and looks into the car.

Lynn answers, "Sir, we are from around here."

And while looking straight ahead focusing on the remains of an insect that had the earlier misfortune of flying head-on into the windshield, Madeline asks, "Is there something wrong officer?"

"Was I talking to you?" he asks.

"No," she replies. "But I—"

"But my ass," he interrupts. "Both of you, get your asses out of the car!"

The sleeve of Lynn's coat gets caught on the handle of the car door as she fumbles around while trying to open it. The enraged policeman snatches the door open before she can get her sleeve free, causing her to fall onto the shoulder of the road. As she scurries to get to her feet, he stands over her, looking down.

"Get your sorry ass on your feet, you bitch, before I lock your sorry ass up," he says.

Madeline jumps out of the car and runs around to the other side to help Lynn. The officer pulls his pistol from its holster and points it at Madeline, causing her to stop dead in her tracks. Still down on her knees and with tears rolling down her face, Lynn screams out, "Why are you doing this to us?"

The officer smiles and says, "Mainly because I can. Do either one of you all got a problem with that? You see, I can tell up-north niggers when I see them. And you two are from up north aren't you? You all bring your do-gooder asses down here and fill these niggers heads full of that "I got rights" bullshit. Yawl tries and tell them what they do and don't have to take off people. But this here is our country, and we run it as I see fit."

Madeline, with both of her hands in the air, slowly explains, "We are both from down here, and if you lower the gun, I will get my purse and show you."

After thinking about it for a moment, he says, "Ok, get your damn purse. But if you're lying, I'm going to blow you and this weeping bitch right here. Right off the face of this planet."

Madeline slowly lowers her hands and walks back around to the passenger side of the car. She then opens the door and reaches into the car. Lying next to her purse is the pouch with Lynn's pistol in it. Madeline hesitates when she sees it.

For a brief moment, she entertains the thought of pulling the pistol from the pouch and showing the large gutted man that he too, can be removed from the face of the planet. She then retrieves the purse, pulls out her driver's license, and hands them to the officer.

By that time, Lynn, still weeping, is standing on her feet. And while the officer looks at her driver's license, Madeline takes Lynn by the hand and pulls her toward her. She then pushes Lynn behind her so that she is standing between Lynn and the officer.

After examining the license, the officer tosses them onto the hood of the car. He takes a bullet from his gun belt, hands it to Lynn, and says, "Here's a little reminder. And if I ever catch either one of you with them troublemakers from up north, it will be the last thing you'll ever do. Now, you all have yourselves a nice and safe trip back to Coffeeville."

He then gets back into his car and drives off while Lynn and Madeline, still traumatized from the encounter, stand motionlessly on the side of the highway.

Chapter 17

THE REALIZATION

As THEY CONTINUE THEIR JOURNEY home, a feeling of anger mixed with pity fills the car, creating an almost suffocating effect. The pity that they feel is not for themselves, nor is it for the four boys that the rogues perpetrating as representatives of justice assaulted and inflicted inhuman indignities upon.

It is for the two officers. For Lynn and Madeline both feel that people who find such joy in trying to destroy another human's self-respect must indeed have no self-esteem for themselves. And that, if they were to allow the actions of these two heartless individuals to dictate how they treat others, it would cast them in the same light.

The deep anger that weighs on them points within. Not because they couldn't do anything to stop the officer from humiliating them. But for not stopping the car and standing up with—and for—the four young men and demanding that they all be treated as human beings.

Or just maybe, the reason for the anger and pity that they feel is the only thing that their inner-self can offer up to compensate for the petrifying fear that prevented them from getting involved. Whichever it is, the incidents will forever be another dark place in their memory for many years to come.

As Lynn and Madeline turn off the main highway and onto the road that leads into Coffeeville, the silence is interrupted.

"I think we should go back to the cave and collect all of the jars and hold them as ransom until that wicked bitch give us our lives back," says Madeline.

After a sigh, Lynn replies, "I think you're right."

And with that, they agree that they should spend the night at Lynn's house, being it is closer and that they should get an early start so that they can get there, do what they need to do, and get back to the house before dark.

"Can I get you anything?" Lynn asks as she pulls her keys out of the door.

"Sure, anything with a kick to it," Madeline answers.

They both sip on soda and bourbon as they gather up the things that they need for the next day. While dreading what could happen once they reenter the den, not going back and leaving things as they are, isn't even an option.

After arriving back at the gas station, they park the car in the back and unload a flashlight, a lantern, two bundles of paper bags, and a large mirror from the trunk. They both know that it will take several trips to remove all of the jars from the den and that it has to be done before nightfall. As they walk through the woods with their arms full, they hardly say a word to each other, until they come upon the field of tall grass.

As they look out beyond the field, they can see the chimney of the little shack.

"This looks like as good a place to rest as any," Lynn says as she plops down on the trunk of a fallen tree. After setting the items that she is carrying onto the ground, Madeline leans up against a tall tree and pulls a cigarette from her pocket.

"You do know that stuff will kill you, don't you?" says Lynn.

Madeline looks down at her, smiles, and replies, "Going back into that cave can kill me as well."

She pulls a box of matches from her pocket and lights the cigarette. After resting for a while, they pick up the bundles and continue their journey.

As they ease up to the edge of the field, they set down their burdens once more and peek out from the shadows of the tall grass to scan the house to see if anyone is standing outside. Once they are sure that the coast is clear, they slowly work their way around to the rear of the house.

Madeline whispers a prayer before scurrying across the open area that lies between the tall grass and the entrance to the shed that covers the opening to the tunnel. The hinges on the decrypted door make a creepy sound that reverberates off of the walls, echoing down the narrow corridor of the shaft. Madeline picks up a piece of wood that is lying on the ground and passes it to Lynn and motions for her to use it to prop open the door.

Slowly and very carefully, they carry the mirror down the steep and narrow steps. After making it to the bottom, they place it so that the light from the sun reflects off of it and shines directly down the corridor of the tunnel. The beam of sunlight is so bright that it looks as if they brought a piece of the sun itself in with them.

As the bats, spiders, and other creatures inhabiting the crevasses of the once-dark passageway scurry about in their attempt to escape the intruding light. Lynn and Madeline duck and cover their heads to protect themselves from hanging cobwebs and the fleeing indwellers. While some of the irritated inhabitant's chooses to flee deeper yet into the tunnel in their attempt to find new and perhaps better places to conceal themselves. A few opt to fly blindly toward the light as the two uneasy intruders ease their way toward the cavern where the jars are kept.

After making the first turn, Lynn and Madeline notice a decrease in the intensity of the light. And by the time they make the last turn, which is just before the straightaway that leads into the cavern, the light being reflected by the mirror is gone, and they find themselves in pitch-black darkness.

Madeline pulls a match from her pocket and lights the lantern. As she adjusts the flame, the tiny eyes of the once-scurrying inhabitants start to reappear as they peep out of the shadows of the entangled roots and hollowed-out burrows of the earth. The tiny specs of reflective light speckle the ceiling of the tunnel like tiny little stars in a pitch-black sky.

Lynn and Madeline both cringe as the tiny creatures screech and hiss while adjusting themselves about in their new roosts. Lynn reaches for the pistol, and in her haste to pull it from her pocket, she chips her fingernail on the handle. The chipped nail snags on her coat pocket, causing her to nearly drop the gun as she pulls it out.

As they inch their way along, they use the walls as a guide while their eyes adjust to the change in the light.

This place seems even creepier than it did the first time we were here, Lynn thinks to herself as they near the threshold of the cavern.

"Do you think that beast is still down here?" Madeline asks in a low voice.

"If it is, I am going to put so many holes in it that it's going to whistle when the wind blows," Lynn replies as they arrive at the entrance.

With her finger on the trigger and the pistol raised, Lynn eases her head around the corner. She sees the many jars that line the shelves and the thick wooden door that closes off the room where the human-like creature was kept. But this time, there are no lighted candles, and the cavern is as dark as the tunnel they traveled through to get there.

As they walk past the altar, Lynn checks behind it to make sure that no one is hiding there. She then makes her way over to the door and peeks through the barbed-wire-covered opening and sees that the chamber is empty, except for some rags that are piled up on the floor in a corner.

Madeline notices a man's wedding ring in one of the jars. She picks up the jar and opens it. Just as Lynn says in a loud pronounced voice, "Ok, let's get started!"

The booming voice not only silences all of the already irritated inhabitants as it echoes about the wall, but also scares Madeline and causes her to drop the ring.

"*Damn*!" says Madeline.

"What's wrong?" asks Lynn.

"I dropped the ring that was in this jar, and now I can't find it," she replies. "I think it hit the floor and rolled." She crawls around on the floor in search of it.

"We don't have a lot of time. Let's get the rest of the stuff out of here, and we will come back and look for it after we're done." Says Lynn.

"Okay!" Madeline replies as she stands to her feet and hands it to Lynn.

She and Madeline then start loading bag after bag with the bottles and jars from the shelves. Once they are done stuffing the bags, they carry them through the tunnel, up the steps, and into the field of tall grass, where they hide them under a big pile of scattered brush—until they can later be moved to the car.

"I am sure glad this is the last trip," says Madeline.

"That makes two of us," Lynn replies as they make their final trip up the narrow stairs.

Chapter 18

THE RACE

By the time they get finished loading and moving the bags, the sun is starting to set, and the cool breeze of the autumn evening is beginning to blow.

"I sure hope we didn't take too much time to finish this," says Lynn.

"So do I," Madeline replies.

While going to retrieve her jacket, which she laid next to the burn barrel that sat on the side of the shack, Lynn sees one of the burlap sacks covering the windows move as if someone has peeked out. She then looks over to where she laid her jacket, which contains in its pockets both the pistol and her wallet. And she sees that it is gone.

"Let's go," she says in an uneasy voice as she starts hurry toward the tall grass.

"What's the matter?" asks Madeline.

"I think someone is watching us from the house," Lynn quickly replies.

"Oh my God!" gasps Madeline as she picks up her pace as well.

Once in the tall grass, Lynn grabs Madeline by the arm and motions for her to squat down. They both turn and look back toward the house. After a moment or two, the old woman comes hobbling out with the frail, human-like creature following close behind, as if it is her little puddle dog. They both head straight for the shack.

As soon as the door on the shack slams shut, Lynn whispers, "Let's go."

Away they run, as fast as their feet can carry them.

"We'll drop this stuff off with the other and head to the car," she continues on to say as they run. After covering them with more brush, they look up at the sun and watch as it slowly descends behind the horizon.

"We don't have a lot of time, and we've got a long way to go, so let's move," Lynn says as they start their journey back to the gas station. Once again, dusk gives way to night, and the stars leisurely start to appear in the darkening sky.

"Listen. Did you hear that?" whispers Madeline.

"Hear what?" Lynn replies.

"There it is again," says Madeline. As they both listen, they can hear twigs snapping and a crunching sound coming from the leaves that cover the forest floor.

They both start running as fast as they can, but the arduous task of moving the jars has taken its toll on them, so they know that they will have to stop soon and rest. No matter how fast they run, whatever follows them seems to be moving even faster.

Soon, the sounds of the snapping twigs are replaced by the sounds of tree branches violently breaking. And the crunching sound from the fallen leaves also becomes more intense. It is as if whatever is following them is not only getting stronger but growing in size as well.

Knowing that they will not be able to keep ahead of it for much longer, they decide to veer off the path and try to find a place to hide.

"There's another path over there," says Madeline. The change of direction is so abrupt that Lynn's feet almost slip from under her as they make the turn.

After only being on the new path for a short time, they come upon a gravel road. The road is dark and overgrown with weeds, but the light from the moon helps lights the route. They look first to the left and then to the right and cannot see where the road leads due to it curving.

"This way!" shouts Lynn as she steps up out of the ditch and onto the road.

Just as they come around the turn, they hear a loud growling and hissing sound coming from behind them. The growling and hissing sound is followed by heavy panting, and the crunching of the leaves is replaced with the sound of claws striking against the densely packed gravel that makes up the unkept road.

The scratching sound is replicated over and over again with a recognizable increase in rhythm. Lynn and Madeline both know that this means that the unknown pursuer has gone from a fast trot to an all-out sprint. The creature releases another loud, growling howl as it closes in. Lynn and Madeline look back over their shoulders and see only the darkness of the night.

"I can't go much farther," cries Madeline as she holds her side to try and ease the pain of the cramps caused by the running.

"We got to keep moving," says Lynn, interlocking her arm with Madeline's. "Look, there's a place to hide over there, just on the other side of those bushes." Lynn pulls Madeline off the road and toward what remains of a burnt-out structure.

Once they have crossed the threshold of the dilapidated, roofless structure, whatever is chasing them stops just short of being in the open, where it could be seen. At first, Lynn thinks they have run into the remains of the burnt-down house. But once inside, it seems more like a small barn with only the remnants of four walls.

They stand on either side of the entryway with their backs against the wall. Scared and tired, they wait silently for whatever it is to enter. After waiting for several long minutes, which seems like forever, nothing happens. Lynn peers through the opening and sees a shadow lurking just beyond the thick brush.

"I don't think it wants us to see it," she whispers. "I can't make out what it is, but it's standing just beyond the thickets over there."

"What do you think we should do?" whispers Madeline.

"Being that it's not trying to get in, at least for now, I think we should just stay here," answers Lynn.

After some time, the moon starts to make its way into the night sky. Its glow casts an eerie light onto the walls and floors of the structure. Madeline begins to ease her way across the entrance toward Lynn. And as soon as she steps out in front of the opening, the thing that had been chasing them lunges from the brush. In just two long strides, it is at the entrance and within striking distance of them.

But for some strange reason, it stops just shy of the entrance and starts to pace back and forth. The horrific creature gestures as if it is ready and willing to dismember and devour them both. But for some reason, it doesn't or can't enter the structure.

It just stands there, making a serpent-like sound through its sharp teeth. Madeline is so petrified that she cannot move a muscle. Because in her mind, she truly believes with all certainty that the end has come.

Lynn gasps and holds her breath as the creature charges. And at that moment she too feels that the end is near. Without thinking, she reaches out across the entrance and pulls Madeline to the ground and out of the creature's sight. They both crawl over to the far side of the structure and position themselves so that they can see the beast through an opening in the wall—but it cannot see them.

As they look on, the partially fur-covered beast growls, hisses, and sniffs around on the ground. For an instant, it stands upright like a man then returns to all fours. Its eight feet of height make it seem, if possible, even more frightening. With its eyes glowing like red pieces of coal, its pointed hairless ears moving ever so slightly as it listens for whatever sound Lynn or Madeline might make.

The sight of its stubby tail wiggling from side to side, as if it has a mind of its own, keeps Madeline's attention for only a few seconds. For, its long claws that extend several inches from the base its paws and their distinct indentation in the earth's soil as it moves about coupled with its sharp spiny-like teeth. Significantly overshadowed any cuteness that might have been associated with the wiggling of the tail.

It drools at the mouth and emits the scent of flesh rotting as it struts around in its relentless pursuit of them. This beast is indeed something that has been summoned from the depths of hell.

After a while, the creature moves out of their line of sight.

"Did you see that?" asks Madeline.

"Yes" whispers Lynn as she raising a finger to her lips as she motion for Madeline to keep her voice down.

"It's huge!" Madeline goes on to say.

"I saw!" Lynn whispers as she continues to motion for Madeline to lower her voice.

Lynn starts searching the ground for something that can be used as a weapon. While looking, she notices something lying under what looks like the seat of an old bench. The item is covered with ash and soot from the apparent fire that seemed to have taken place many, many years ago, but the light from the moon makes it shine.

She reaches down, moves the charred bench, and picks up a relatively large golden cross. The cross is about ten inches long with a small chain attached to it. All four of its arms end in a point, and it bears an inscription written in Latin .

"Find something?" asks Madeline.

"Yes. It looks like a cross of some sort. And it looks and feels like it's made of solid gold," she answers.

Then, without warning, the hideous creature suddenly appears at the window next to where Madeline is sitting. Madeline cringes as she presses her back against the wall. And in one swift motion, it sticks its ugly head through the window frame and growls through its sharp teeth as it sniffs the air for their scent. With saliva dripping from its mouth, it peers side to side as it looks for them.

After a second or so, the skin on the creature's hideous face start to smoke and then bubble as if it is somehow being cooked. The beast then quickly withdraws its smoldering head from the window and releases a whimpering sound, like something a dog would make, as it retreats back into the thickets.

It all happened so quickly that neither Lynn nor Madeline had time to respond.

"Do you think it saw us?" asks Madeline.

"No, I don't think so. Did you see the bubbles on its face?" asks Lynn.

Madeline nods.

Chapter 19

A SANCTUARY

As THE COLD NIGHT AIR settles in, the beast eases its way back out into the open, where it can be seen. Steam rises from its nostrils with each breath it exhales. It paces back and forth for a period and then lies down on a pile of dry leaves as if it is bedding down for the night.

Lynn and Madeline continue to watch the beast until their view is gradually obstructed by a dense fog that slowly rolls over the entire area. At one point, the fog gets so thick that they can only see a few yards in front of them. As they cautiously gather whatever dry wood they can find within the structure to build a fire, they keep watch for the beast.

After building a warm fire, they huddle together in front of it. The heat from the flames is a welcome delight to their cold and trembling bodies. They sit down next to each other and talk about things, like how good life is going to be once Willie and David get well and how they are going to tell them each and every day how much they love and care for them.

Lynn talks about her children. She tells Madeline about how supportive they are and how she doesn't think she would have made it as far as she has if it weren't for them. Madeline, in turn, talks about her other son Sonny. Telling Lynn about how hard it is for him to accept what is happening with his brother David.

And as the fog becomes still and the conversation tapers, the realities of the present situation start to settle back in. The reality of the monstrous creature waiting just beyond the walls to do God knows what to them at any given moment. And the fact that Willie and David might not ever get well or could die before the next sunrise.

As these thoughts rush through their minds, it becomes almost too much for them to bear. And as the tears start to once again roll down their faces, Lynn reminds Madeline of why they are there.

"We're doing this because of Willie and David," she says. "And if you or I was lying in that hospital in their place. I think, no! I know that they would be out here doing exactly what we are doing. I know that things are not what we want them to be, but if we give up now, they will have nobody."

She then leans her back against the wall and wipes the tears from her face as they both stare into the flames.

As the night grows long, their minds tell them that it is not wise to go to sleep. So in a heartfelt attempt to stay awake, they try to encourage each other by repeating the words "We can do this! We can do this!" However, it has been a long and hard day, and their tired bodies do not agree. Soon, they are both in a deep slumber.

A drop of dew falls from the night sky, striking Madeline on the forehead, causing her to wake up from an uneasy sleep. As she looks around, she sees that the fog has somewhat lifted and that she is now able to see out past the walls of the structure. She stretches then eases her way over to the window seal and looks out to see that the creature has gone.

She then looks over at Lynn. Lynn mumbles and turns, still in her restless sleep. At first, she starts to wake her up, but after giving it a second thought, she decided not to. *Even restless sleep beats no sleep at all*, Madeline thinks to herself.

The wind makes an eerie hum as it blows around the jagged edges of the walls and through the window frames of the structure. As Madeline listens, the eerie hum starts to sound more and more like someone's crying for help. At first, it's not clear, and it sounds as if the cry is a long way away. But the more she listens, the closer and clearer it becomes.

"Help! Help! Help…"

She walks over to the other side of the structure, where it sounds like it is coming from, and looks out through a window facing an old cemetery.

She gazes out over the broken and leaning tombstones and sees what first looks like a thick patch of fog with a small whirlwind winding it up. And while she watches, the piece of fog slowly turns into a small child beckoning for help.

"Help! Help! Help…" whispers the wind as she strains her eyes to see if it's all an illusion or if it's truly someone in need of help.

Madeline looks over at Lynn once more and sees that she's still in her restless and tormented sleep. She then turns and focuses her attention back on what's happening in the cemetery. She rubs her eyes and tries to concentrate as she strains to make out the humanoid figure that beckons for her help. *Is this truly a child, or is it something that I'm imagining?* she ponders.

The more she watches it, the more real the image becomes. And soon it is as clear as a bright star in a dark night sky. And she's able to see exactly what it is in great detail. The once-whirling fog has become a small girl whose legs are tangled in some tree branches.

Madeline is able to make out all of the child's facial features, except for the eyes. She sees her long-braided pigtails with black ribbons flowing in the wind as the fog slowly blows across the tombstones. She sees the color of the lace on her bright white dress and even the color of her nail polish.

With the calls for help ringing in her ears and the sight of the child beckoning for her assistance, Madeline feels that she has to act and act fast if she was going to help the child before the creature returns. As her adrenaline levels increase and the question of "What should I do?" races around in her head, she makes the decision to go for it.

She quickly makes her way back over to the door and looks out and sees that the creature has not returned. She then runs back over to the window facing the cemetery and sees that the child is still there. After taking a deep breath, she steps up onto the window seal and looks to her left and then to her right. After making sure that the coast is clear, she jumps.

Before her feet reach the ground, she's snatched back into the structure and lands flat on her back. After landing on the ground, faceup, she sees Lynn with her arms around her, lying on the ground next to her.

"What in the hell are you doing?" asks Lynn.

"I am trying to save that child out there that's stuck and calling for help," she replies. "What child?" asks Lynn.

"The one that's standing right over there," says Madeline as she stands up and points out across the cemetery.

And right before their eyes, the beautiful little girl changes into the hideous she-devil Althea. And within seconds, she is joined by the monstrous beast. With the creature by her side, Althea releases a scream that is so ghostly, it silences all of the nightly sounds of the forest.

Chapter 20

THE MORNING AFTER

For the remainder of the night, the woods echo with the sounds of a haunting. At times, it sounds as if someone has unleashed a horde of screaming banshees. The thunderous clamor of breaking branches and cries from the captured souls pulsates as if they are being summoned from the threshold of hell itself as Althea and the monstrous creature search for her horde .

The almost-endless screams and cries go on until just before the break of dawn. Then it all slowly fades away. It is as if Althea and the beast moved just fast enough to keep ahead of daylight. As the fog clears, the birds greet the morning with chirps and chatters as they gossip with one another about the events of the night.

Lynn and Madeline squat close to the remnants of a once-cracking fire, staring at the ashes.

"Do you think it's safe enough for us to leave yet?" asks Madeline once the sun has made its way over the treetops.

"I think so. But first, let's finish what we came here to do," Lynn replies.

Lynn picks up a large stick from off of the ground and swings it like a baseball player swings his bat.

"This should work," she mumbles after a few swings.

"And what in the world are you planning on doing with that?" asks Madeline.

"You do know that thing will probably use that stick to pick its teeth after it finishes eating us," she continues on to say.

Lynn doesn't say a word as she peeks out the door. And with the stick drawn back, she steps across the threshold.

As they walk back through the brush and step onto the road, they both look back at the structure that served as their sanctuary from the devilish crusaders. Neither say a word, for the light of day allows them to see the structure in its entirety. With its brunt-off roof and its crumbled walls, the tiny structure stands firm against the foes who dare to lay siege on its walls.

Pretty much hidden from the world—yet fate, or maybe just plain luck, led Lynn and Madeline to the warmth and security of its inner cavity. Is it just an old shed or burnt-out barn that has given them refuge? Or maybe it is what remains of a dilapidated house, like they once thought. Whatever it once was, neither knows or cares because, to them, it is now and forever known as the place that stood strong when options where none.

"Be careful," Lynn says as they navigate through the trees and broken branches that litter the road. And as they look around, the broken branches and uprooted trees make it obvious where Althea and the creature searched. The devastation left in the aftermath of their search is not only frightening but a testimony to the beast's physical strength as well.

After making their way back to where they hid the items, they decide that it would be best to move everything into the structure. It takes several trips for them to move all of the bags, but they do not dare stop and rest until they are done.

"I think this is going to be a pretty day," Madeline says in her effort to make conversation as they drive back to Lynn's house.

"Yes, it does seem like it," Lynn replies.

"I see that you still have the dreams," says Madeline.

"Each and every time I close my eyes," answers Lynn.

"What exactly are they about?" Madeline asks.

After a brief pause , Lynn answers, "At first, I thought they were something evil, but now I'm not so sure."

"What happened that changed your mind?" Madeline asks.

"Well, remember last night when you were about to go out into that cemetery?"

"Yes," answers Madeline.

"The man in the dream awakened me," Lynn says.

"How can a person in a dream wake somebody up?" Madeline asks.

Lynn senses a trace of disbelief from the tone of Madeline's voice as she goes on to say, "He didn't actually say wake up or shake me or anything like that. He just stood there with both of his arms extended as if he was trying to get me to stand up and come to him. After standing up, I opened my eyes, and there you were. Standing on the window seal."

Chapter 21

A BROKEN SHUTTER

ONCE AT HOME, LYNN NERVOUSLY walks into the house and turns on the living-room light. With her mind still engulfed with the events that took place over the last forty-eight hours, she eases her way through the empty house, searching and turning on the lights in each and every room, like a child who is looking for the ever-so-elusive boogie man.

I have got to pull myself together, she thinks as she walks back into the bedroom and turns down the bed. After starting a fire in the fireplace, she goes into the bathroom and starts filling the bathtub. As the tub fills, she pulls the gold cross from her pocket and washes it off in the sink.

After undressing, she pours herself a glass of milk and then eases her body into the tub of warm water. As she takes a sip of the milk, she examines the cross, and she tries disparately to rationalize the things that are going on in her life. The more she thinks about it, the more bizarre it all seems.

After a long soaking bath, she readies herself for bed. She sticks the cross under the pillow and then goes back into the front room and calls Howard to see how the children are doing. As soon as Howard answers the phone, she hears the children in the background cheerfully pleading to speak with her. Howard quickly says his hellos and passes the phone on to them. After talking to them for more than an hour, she asks them to put their uncle back on the phone.

"How has everything been going?" he asks. "I was starting to get worried because we haven't heard from you in the last couple of days. Is everything Ok?"

Not wanting to upset anyone, she downplays the events of the past couple of days by saying that she has been so busy that she hasn't had time to call. And that she will probably be headed that way sometime in the next few days if nothing comes up. After a brief conversation about Willie and the kids' grades, they say their goodbyes. Lynn then hangs up the phone and goes to bed.

Not long after falling asleep, she starts to dream once more. In this dream, she and the unknown stranger are sitting in a small boat on a large lake, with the shoreline in the far distance. At first, the water is calm, and the air is still. Then without warning, thing rapidly start to change. The water begins to toss the small craft from side to side as the wind commences howling like a bloodhound that just picked up the scent of its prey.

All of a sudden, there is a loud bang. And the stranger disappears into thin air, leaving her all alone. While still staring at the spot where the stranger once sat, she notices a cigarette lighter lying on the seat. As she stands up and tries to walk over to pick it up, a massive wave hits the side of the boat, causing it to capsize.

Lynn covers her face as she readies herself for the impact of the water. But she doesn't land in the turbulent waters; her eyes open, and she find herself sweating profusely and lying faceup in her bed. After lying motionless for a moment or two, she sits up and reaches over and turns on the lamp.

Another loud banging sound rings out, followed by the sounds of strong winds whistling through whatever opening in the house that they can find. Lynn turns and looks at the clock and sees that it's 12:24 a.m. She then places both feet onto the floor, slips into her house shoes, stands up, stretches, and walks over to the window and looks out.

The light from the moon intermittently peeks through the window as a patchy, slow-rolling fog makes its way across the landscape. The gradual and involuntary movement of the fog and the life like movement of the trees seem to obey the many commands given by the forces of the gusty winds as they push and pull them in all directions. Even the shadow from the loose shutter seems to move in unison with the trees as it slams up against the house time and time again. Lynn flinches ever so slightly with each bang from the shutter while looking out at fog.

As the fog becomes broader and denser, the tapping sound from the rain hitting the windows intensifies. It soon becomes impossible to see more than a few yards or so from the house as the heavier rains bring with them enormous flashes of lighting and the intense sounds of rolling thunder.

Lynn walks back over to the bed, sits down, and reaches over to turn off the lamp. But just as she raised her arm, there is another bright flash of lighting, followed by the loudest clap of thunder yet. Then the house goes dark.

"Damn! The electricity is out," she mutters to herself as she turns and lays her back against the pillows.

While lying there, she sees the lighting intermittently flash through the thick patches of fog, casting the shadows of the trees into the house and onto the bedroom walls. As the shadows dance about the room, she watches on in silence. Finding it hard to get back to sleep with all the ghostly figures moving about the room, she gets up and closes the curtain. And with the passing of only a few short minutes, she is back off to sleep.

As the storm and the daunting winds retreat, the banging noise from the loose shutter is soon replaced with an eerie dead silence.

"Lynn. Lynn. Lynn…" a voice whispers, breaking the silence of her sleep. Lynn slowly opens her eyes, unable to tell if the voice is a reality or part of a dream as she loiters somewhere between sleep and consciousness.

As the voice fades into silence, she wipes her face. And as her eyes focus, she sees the light of the moon flashing through the small opening between the curtains. Like a flash from the lighting, it too casts the shadow of the trees onto the bedroom walls. She sits up in the bed and looks over at the clock and sees that it's 3:48 a.m.

She then tries to turn on the lamp once more. "Damn! The power is still out!" she mumbles with disgust once more. After a stretch, she gets up and walks over to the window and opens the curtains.

As the curtains open, the window comes crashing in on her. The force is so great that she is knocked across the room, landing faceup on the bed. She looks up, and there stands the enormous creature from the night before. Althea and the beastly creature have spent almost the entire night searching for them and the items that they took from the cave.

Lynn screams and tries to make it to the other side of the bed. But it is too late. The creature pounces on her within seconds of crashing through the window. It clamps its mighty jaws around her left leg. And as the sharp teeth dig into her flesh, she desperately reaches for the bedpost to try and pull herself away from its deadly grip.

The beast drags her frail body from the bed onto the floor as she clings to the bed linen, pulling it along with her. In her effort to escape, she reaches for the bedpost once more but falls short, grabbing the pillow instead. As she releases the pillow and tries again, her hand lands on the cross that she put underneath the pillows.

In one final, desperate motion, she swings the cross and embeds in the creature's eye socket forcing it to release her leg and go into an erratic frenzy. As the creature dies, Lynn shakes as she crawls into a corner of the room and curls her body into a ball.

As soon as the creature's body becomes motionless, it changes momentarily into a young man, then it turns to dust as the sun once more makes its way over the horizon. At a distance, the grieving wails from Althea can be heard fading off into the countryside.

Chapter 22

AMOS KOONS

As LYNN SITS CURLED UP in the corner of the room, she rocks back and forth, her mind nearing the state of break-down. She not only struggles to accept the life-and-death confrontation that she had just had with the creature, but also tries to rationalize the dreams of her and the stranger. Especially the one with them on the small boat.

"What is it about this dream?" she asks herself as she replays it over and over again in her mind. Then like a spark in the night, it comes to her. "It's the cigarette lighter!" she whispers to herself. She then recalls seeing one just like it inside one of the jars, dent and all.

She also remembers that Willie once carried a similar lighter back when he smoked. But she can't remember if it was dented or not. *Could that be Willie's lighter in the jar?* she wonders. *I need to get that lighter.*

She then gets up and runs into the other room, where the phone is, and calls Madeline. After several rings, Madeline answers, "Hello?"

From the sound of her voice, Lynn can tell that she has awakened her and that Althea must not have found her during the night.

"Hello, Madeline. Get dressed and come over. I need to see you right away," Lynn quickly explains.

"What's wrong?" Madeline asks.

"I will explain when you get here. Hurry!" she says.

Shortly after she hangs up the phone, there is a knock at the door. She grabs her housecoat and puts it on as she goes to answer it. Once at the door, she peeks out and sees that it's their neighbor, Amos Koons. He waves as he sees her looking out at him.

"Good morning!" he says as she peeks around the partly opened door.

"Good morning, Mr. Koons," she replies.

"Looks like we really had a bad one last night," he says. "Looks like you've got quite a bit of damage around back too?"

"Yes, I know!" answers Lynn.

"I got a few pieces of plywood out in back of my house. If you like, I'll cover that window opening up for you," he says.

"That would be wonderful," Lynn replies, smiling. While Amos goes to get his tools and the plywood needed to board up the window, Lynn quickly bandages her leg and gets dressed.

Amos Koons is an elderly, thin-framed Caucasian gentleman who sports a short, rough-looking beard and walks with a slight limp. He often brags that the limp is from an injury that he received while performing one of his many heroic deeds back while fighting in the war. He is looked upon by many of the local Whites as somewhat of a social outcast, partly because of his relationship with the Negroes and the few Indians that remain in the area. But the main reason is because of his attitude toward them.

His loathing of the locals started shortly before he returned from the war, when he received a letter from his mother notifying him of his father's untimely death. In the letter, she explained that his father was killed while trying to stop the lynching of a Black man who had been accused of inciting the Black community. Amos's father was a small-time minister who had moved to the Delta around the turn of the century to minister to what remained of the once-sizable Indian population, along with a small portion of the Black community.

His mother became so distraught from her husband's death that she eventually took her own life before he could make it home; so he was told. Ever since, he has lived in their house. Some try to make fun of his last name behind his back and joke that the name Koons was given to him because of his association with the Negro community—and they just changed the C into a K. And others joke that it was because of his love of hunting and eating raccoons. Whichever one it is, the name stuck, and after a while, he started to answer to it.

But in his presence, they all knew that you could think whatever you wanted to about the origin of the name; the mister had better come first. Any deviation would probably get you shot. And depending on who you were, maybe shot dead.

This is something that the Whites and Negros alike know well from the numerous accounts about what happened to people who found themselves in compromising situations after crossing him. You see, Mr. Koons has a knack for knowing just when to catch his enemies alone and vulnerable. No witnesses, no crime.

The Mister part is something that the Negros and the Indians don't mind using out of respect for what his father tried to do for them. But the fact is, he prefers that they just call him Amos and will often correct them when they call him Mr. Koons.

Madeline pulls up in front of the house and immediately notices all the scattered debris. The first thing that pops into her head is that Althea must have found Lynn. As she gets out of the car, she hears the hammering sound from Amos nailing the plywood over what once was a window. She walks around back and sees him standing on a short ladder, holding the plywood up with one hand and holding the hammer in the other.

He looks down at her with several nails in his mouth and mumbles, "Good morning!" Madeline, with a puzzled look on her face, replies in kind and then asks, "Where's Lynn, and who are you?"

Amos smiles and motions for Madeline to give him a second or two as he finishes hammering down one of the nails.

He removes the nails from his mouth and says, "I'm Amos," as he steps down off of the ladder and reaches out to shake her hand. Madeline cautiously accepts the handshake and repeats the question: "Where is Lynn?"

"She's in the house, I believe," he answers.

Just then, Lynn opens the back door and sticks her head out. "I thought I heard you talking to someone," she says.

She then tries to introduce Madeline and Mr. Koons to each other but is interrupted by Madeline saying that they have already met.

"Can I get you anything, Mr. Koons?" asks Lynn as she motions for Madeline to come inside.

"Oh no, I have already had breakfast. I'm fine" replies Amos.

Once inside, she offers Madeline a seat at the kitchen table and pours her a cup of coffee.

"As you can probably see, I had visitors last night," She says as she hands the coffee to Madeline.

"How did they find you?" asks Madeline.

"My wallet and the gun were in the pocket of the jacket that was taken while we were in the tunnel," Lynn replies. She then tells Madeline what happened during the night.

She tells her how the fog rolled in just like it did at the burnt out structure and how the man in her dreams awakened her once more when danger was near. She then tells her how she killed the beast with the cross and how it changed into a young man just prior to becoming ashes. Once she has finished, Madeline shakes like a leaf, for she knows that she is probably next on Althea's list.

Chapter 23

THE UNHOLY NIGHT

AFTER TAKING A MOMENT TO compose herself, Lynn adds the part about the cigarette lighter. She tells Madeline that she remembers seeing a dented lighter in one of the jars. She feels that her dreams have something to do with the items in the jars.

As they talk, Lynn notices that the banging of Amos's hammer has stopped. She then turns and looks toward the door. And there he stands. Madeline hasn't noticed the silencing of the hammering, nor does she see him standing in the door as she continues on with the conversation. Lynn clears her throat and slightly tilts her head toward the door after getting Madeline's attention.

"As soon as I heard that howling noise last night, I knew exactly what it was," Amos Koons says as he walks through the back door and into the kitchen. "Even though it tried to mask its cries within the noises of the blowing winds, it was still as distinct and as clear as the sound of a familiar voice.

"It's the sort of sound that, once you hear it, you never forget where it came from. Or worst yet, what makes it. And it makes no difference how much time has passed since you last heard it. You still know," he says, shaking his head.

"It's the same sound I heard as a child many years ago as my mother and I hid in the bushes, along with the other women and children, while my father's church burned to the ground. It raised above all of the yelling and screaming that was going on that night. Men dressed in white sheets, some on horseback, beat and tortured those that were unable or unwilling to escape into the woods.

"It continued on long after the screaming and yelling had given way to soft wails and whimpers of grief and the fire had died down to just a smoldering heap of glowing embers. It finally stopped just before dawn as we were returning to gather up the injured and dead.

"We found my father lying out back of the church. He was severely beaten and had a broken arm. His friend Thomas wasn't there that night, but he showed up early the next morning as we were gathering up the dead and injured.

"I remember Thomas and my dad having an argument about something while Thomas was helping load him into the back of our wagon. After that, Thomas got on his horse and rode off. I later learned that two of the men who were part of the group that attacked and burned the church were found shot to death. It was rumored among some people that Thomas had done it. But there wasn't any proof.

"A few days later, some of the grief-stricken church people who had lost loved ones decided to go and visit the old woman that lived down on the creek. At that time, some believed that she had the power to heal and, in some cases, even bring back the dead for a price.

"By the time my father found out about it, it was too late. They had already started coming down with all sorts of strange illnesses, and some just seemed to have vanished from the face of the earth. After learning what was happening, my father and Thomas went to see the old woman to try and get her to undo what she had done, but nothing came of it. The next day, Thomas's barn was set on fire by the Klan. He lost his wife, Irene, that night. He, too, soon disappeared.

"Some years later, after I had gotten older, I asked my dad about that night and the things that took place shortly after. It was then that he told me about the old woman and others like her. The things that he told me that day I have remembered, and probably will continue to remember, for the rest of my life.

"He said that there were some creatures out there that are even eviler than the people that did those horrible things at the church that night. These creatures feed and survive off of the weaknesses and misfortunes of men and women. The strength of these creatures is enhanced by our prejudices, intolerances, and our exploitation of one another.

"These wicked abominations of man can smell a good and clean soul that's grieving or caught up in some unfortunate dilemma from miles away. And they will do anything, including bartering, haggling, or stealing to add to their coffers. The larger the cache of souls, the stronger they become."

"How do they get one's soul?" asks Lynn.

"I have never personally dealt with one, but I heard that, whenever a person truly gives something to someone, in essence, they are giving a part of themselves," says Amos. "And when a gift is given from anywhere other than the heart…"

"It may very well be the heart," Lynn interrupts.

"That's right," says Amos. "How did you know that?"

Lynn replies, "We met the old lady that lives down on the creek, and she told us to bring all of the jars from the cave to her so she would help us."

"What cave? What jars?" Amos asks. "You mean to tell me that you ladies have entered one of their dens and survived?"

Lynn and Madeline then tell him the entire story.

"What's the purpose of the items in the jars?" asked Madeline.

Amos puts some chew into his mouth and answers, "My father said that they keep the things that they get from people because that is what the souls are attached to. And I guess, as the soul gets used up, the item becomes that powdery stuff."

"You mean to tell me that that dust is all that remains of a person's soul?" Madeline asks. "Yes, I would imagine so," Amos answers.

As he continues with his story, Lynn and Madeline sit and listen.

"And if, for some reason, one of them happens to lose its hoard of souls, it will go to any length to regain them. The longer that it goes without having them, the weaker it becomes in its ability to maintain its human likeness and its powers of manipulation.

"The reason she told you to bring the jars to her was that there are only so many souls to be had in a given area, so they are forced to compete for territory. And if she can get you to bring her the hoard of another, that will make her all the stronger and help diminish the competition." "But she said that she would help us," responds Lynn.

"Remember what you are dealing with here. These are not beings, and they don't have feelings like you or I do. These are soulless entities that are trapped between the threshold of hell and earth. And the only reason that they interact with you is to get a shot at stealing your salvation or the salvation of someone close to you. They long to fill the void of not having one of their own.

"She cannot and will not release a soul. It's not in their nature. They are in the business of collecting them, not freeing them. And if you try to make a deal with her, she will, without a doubt, wind up with your soul in her coffers as well."

Amos opens the kitchen door and spits the chew of tobacco from his mouth onto the ground.

"If you know what items in which jars belong to Willie and David, we need to remove those items from the jars and replace them with something else. In essence, swapping someone else's soul for theirs."

"What if we don't replace them with anything?" Madeline asks.

"Then Althea will probably haunt Willie and David for the remainder of their natural lives, or until they regain their cache of souls—because she now feels that their souls belong to her," Amos replies.

Chapter 24

A COLD WINTER MORNING

Lynn asks Amos, "How did your father come to know that guy Thomas?"

He replies, "When my parents first moved to Mississippi, Thomas was one of the first to befriend them. At the time, I was just five years old, and my mother was pregnant with my sister. We had little or no money at that time.

"It was one of the coldest winter mornings that I can remember. And it had snowed several inches the night before. We were heading to my father's new church, which was just on the other side of Charleston, when the wheel broke off of our wagon.

"My father was trying to fix it, but he didn't have any tools, and frankly, had he had the tools, he probably couldn't have fixed it because he wasn't very good with his hands," Amos says with a chuckle. "I've lived for a long time, and to this day, I don't think that I have ever been as cold as I was that day. Thomas must have seen our wagon from his house that was on the other side of the field.

"Up until that moment, I had never actually seen a Black man close up before. But I was sure glad to see him, especially when he started pulling them warm heavy quilts from his wagon. He then invited us to stay with him and his wife for the night. It sure felt good waking up the next morning to the smell of homemade biscuits.

"After we got settled in at our place, Thomas and his wife, Irene, would come to visit us, or we would go visit them at least once a week. Soon he and my dad became best friends. They helped each other work their fields, and Thomas even showed my dad how to fix things, like the wagon wheels, for instance.

"It seemed like they were always together. A lot of the White people had a problem with it, but my father was his own man. And he didn't care. He would always say, 'God made us all the same; he just kept some in the oven longer than others.'

"Shortly after the burning of our church, I remember, late one night, Thomas coming to our house. My parents sent my sister and me to bed, but I could tell that something was terribly wrong because I saw tears rolling down Thomas's face as he repeatedly said, 'Irene, Irene. My Irene!' And that was the last time that I saw Thomas.

"A few months later, my little sister came down with pneumonia, and the doctor told my folks that there was a good chance that she wasn't going to make it. I was devastated. My sister and I were so close, and I loved her so much that I couldn't stop crying. My father knew that all that crying would only make me sick too, so after some time, he started getting on me about it. After that, I started hiding in the kitchen pantry on those days that I just couldn't hold it in.

"One day, while I was hiding in the pantry, my parents came into the kitchen and started talking. Not knowing that I was there, they spoke of the old woman that lived on the other side of the creek. From the sound of the conversation, my mother wanted to go and see the woman about my sister, but my dad called the woman an abomination of God and said that she was a devil that dealt in the thievery of souls.

"He also said that he had begged Thomas not to go and see her because she was wicked. But Thomas wouldn't listen. He then said something that made the hair on the back of my neck stand up. He said that Thomas had told him that Irene came to see him at night and that she was trying to tell him something."

The more Amos talks about the pass, the more emotional he becomes. His voice starts to crack as he speaks of his father. "They shot him and tied his body to the tree that the lynched man hang from," he says.

"Three days had passed before anybody found him. And once they found him, they sent someone to fetch my mother so that she could identify the body. I was told that the animals had gotten to it and that he could hardly be recognized. I know it took all that Mama had to walk up to that body; it was just too much for her to bear."

Amos then pulls a small medicine bottle from his pocket and shakes it. The container makes a rattling noise .

"What's in there?" Lynn asks.

"These are the bullets that they removed from his body. I found them among Mama's things. I've been carrying them around in my pocket ever since," he answers. "I've lied awake many a night thinking about what I would do to the people that committed that atrocious act on my family. If I ever found out who they were…I guess that must not have been part of God's plan."

"Amos, you're too good a person to downgrade yourself with something as senseless as revenge. Besides, I'm sure that they will probably get just what they deserve if they haven't already," Lynn replies. "I think I know what happened to Thomas."

She starts to tell him the story her grandmother told her about the young couple.

Chapter 25

HOPEFUL REVENGE

AFTER AMOS HAS FINISHED BOARDING up the window, Lynn and Madeline decide that they had better return to the place where they hid the items and figure out what to do with them. After a brief discussion, they decide that Lynn should stay with Madeline until things are resolved.

As they load the last suitcase into the trunk of the car, they hear a voice call out, "Wait for me!"

It is Amos Koons hobbling down the road. He has his double-barrel shotgun in one hand and a box of bullets in the other.

"Mind if I tag along?" he asks as he walks up.

"Sure, glad to have you along," Lynn replies with a smile.

As they drive, Amos talks almost nonstop for most of the ride. Then suddenly, he gets somewhat withdrawn as they near the old gas station. Noticing the change in his demeanor, Lynn asks, "What's wrong, Amos? Cat got your tongue?"

"No," he replies as he rubs his hand across his beard. "There was once an old road that ran right down through where that gas station now sits. I walked that old road many a day with my father back when I was a child. I haven't dared to come out here since my parents died."

Once out of the car, they walk to the back of the gas station and head down the path toward the burnt-down structure. After walking the trail for only a short time, Amos takes the lead. Because by then, he has figured out, what old burnt-out structure they were talking about.

As they walk up to what they now know was once Amos Koons fathers church, Lynn and Madeline say nothing, for they can see that, if they are going to deal with the demons of today, Mr. Koons needs some time to deal with the demons of yesterday.

After gathering up all of the bags containing the jars, they painstakingly haul them through the woods and to the car. Once they have finished loading them, they sit inside the car with the doors open to rest.

"So…where is this den located?" Amos asks.

"It's about an hour or so walk from here," Madeline answers as she pulls a cigarette from her purse and lights it.

Lynn quickly responds, "I know you're not thinking about going there, are you?"

Amos replies, "You said that she's a harmless old woman during the day, didn't you? And besides, if we have to deal with her, I sure as hell want to do it on our terms."

Lynn looks over at Madeline. Madeline hunches her shoulders and says, "He does have a point."

Shotgun in hand , Amos Koons, along with Lynn and Madeline, heads back down the trail. Lynn reiterates the point that they have to be back in the car and gone before dark. After her saying it for the third time, Amos and Madeline jokingly interrupt by saying in unison, "We know…We got to be back at the car and on the road before dark."

Lynn shakes her head and mumbles an obscenity under her breath.

Once they arrive at the edge of the tall grass, the conversation turns back to the task at hand. When Lynn asks, "What are we going to do when we see Althea?" Mr. Koons answer is primitive yet simple: "I'm going to blast her with a couple of loads of buckshot."

After crossing the field, Amos works his way up to the front door of the shack and kicks it open. He then rushes inside while Lynn and Madeline lie and wait at the edge of the field. After several minutes without gunshots, they cautiously walk up to the door. As Madeline and Lynn peak in, they see Amos walking across the room . "She's not here," he says as he steps back onto the porch.

"You think she might be down in the tunnel?" Lynn asks.

"Let's take a look and see," Amos replies as he takes off in the direction of the tunnel. As they descend into the eerie passageway once more, recollection of their previous visits starts to occupy Lynn and Madeline's minds. Amos, who has never faced Althea or her now-deceased minion before, knows not what to fear.

Madeline picks up and lights one of the lanterns sitting on the ground at the entrance just on the other side of the door. As they slowly journey into the damp cavern, they look for any signs and listen for any sound that might indicate Althea's presence.

While the creepy occupants of the nooks and crannies screech and scurry to conceal themselves, Lynn, Amos, and Madeline make their way down the dark corridor. After traveling about halfway, Lynn pauses and signals for everyone to stop what they are doing and listen. Standing as still as statues, they listen and try to navigate the hissing and screeching sounds of the tiny, irritated inhabitants and the sound of something happening down the corridor behind them.

Amos takes the lantern from Madeline and walks back down the corridor to see if anyone is coming up from behind them. He is only gone for a short while. On his return, he tells them that the coast is clear, and they continue their journey.

Shortly after that, they find themselves at the entrance of the den. The den is still in disarray from when they were there before. Amos sets the lantern on a high shelf by the entrance so that the light can illuminate the entire room.

While Madeline shows Amos the shelving where the jars once sat, Lynn walks over to the room where the creature was kept. As she looks down at the floor, she sees her jacket, balled up and lying in the corner. It is as if the old lady used it to give the beast her scent. She quickly reaches down, picks it up, and searches the pockets for her pistol and wallet.

Not finding either item, she walks over to the altar. As she looks at the altar, she sees her wallet and all of the things that was in it sprawled out and surrounded by several melted candles. As she starts to gather up her belongings, she notices a piece of paper on the floor next to the altar. When she bends down to pick up the piece of paper, she finds the ring that Madeline dropped when they were last there.

After picking up the piece of paper, she sees that it's the same piece of paper that she had written the address of Willie's hospital on.

The wicked woman now knows where Willie is. And for Willie's sake, they have to hurry up and get there.

Chapter 26

THE RACE

"WE NEED TO GO!" SHOUTS Lynn.

"What's wrong?" Madeline asks as she walks over to see what it is that Lynn is holding in her hand. Just as Lynn shows her the piece of paper, the near silence is suddenly broken with a blast from Amos's shotgun.

With the temporary loss of hearing caused the discharge of the shotgun, Lynn and Madeline can only see that Amos is yelling something but cannot hear what he is saying. Amos, realizing that they can't hear him, waves his arm, motioning for them to duck down behind the altar. No sooner have they ducked, the lantern comes flying across the cavern and explodes into flames as it smashes against the wall.

Amos unleashes another blast from the shotgun and then yells for Lynn and Madeline to follow him as he rushes through the exit. Even before the ringing in their ears has stopped, they know exactly what Amos was shooting at. For the cries that echo through the cavern are the same cries that have been indefinitely etched into their memory. Althea has returned!

"Amos!" Lynn shouts as they try to catch up to him. But the farther away they get from the burning den, the darker it gets and the farther they fall behind. Soon Lynn and Madeline find themselves in pitch darkness. As they feel their way along the wall, Madeline pulls her lighter from her pocket and lights it.

For a while, they can still hear the faint sounds of Amos's boots, stomping against the ground as he runs. But they, too, soon fade away, leaving complete and utter silence.

"No matter what happens, hang on," Lynn says as she reaches down and takes Madeline by the hand.

"She had us. Why did she run?" Madeline asks.

"Because it's like the old woman said. Without her mass of stolen souls, her power is minimal. And I sure hope Amos is able to get her before she gets away," Lynn replies as they slowly continue feeling their way through the darkness.

Soon, they're able to see a sliver of light coming from the cracks around the door at the entrance of the tunnel. As Lynn pushes the door open, they see Amos sitting on the back steps of the shack.

"Well, did you get her?" Lynn asks.

And as she steps across the threshold and into the daylight, Amos replies, "No! It's almost like she vanished into thin air as soon as she stepped out of the door. I couldn't have been more than twenty paces behind her."

"Where do you think she could have gone?" Madeline asks.

"I don't know, but I do know exactly where she's headed the first chance she gets, and that is to find Willie and

David!" Lynn stammers. She then shows Madeline and Amos the piece of paper. "And we've got to beat her there," she continues.

Amos makes one more search around the parameter of the house before they all head back to the car. As they disappear into the tall grass, the succubus steps away from the side of the shack. And like a chameleon lizard, she transforms herself back into her human-like color and texture.

The long walk back to the gas station is done at a rapid pace and with very few words spoken, for they all know that they have to hurry up and get on the road if they are going to beat Althea to David and Willie. As they exit the path and walk toward the rear of the gas station, Amos excuses himself to go take a bathroom break. Madeline and Lynn continue on to the front where the car is located. As they step around the corner, they both stop dead in their tracks.

To their surprise, Althea is squatting down beside the car.

Lynn impulsively yells out, "What in the hell are you doing?"

Althea turns and punctures one of the car tires with a long, sharp knife. She then rises to her feet and starts coming toward them.

Backing away, Lynn and Madeline can see what the toll of not having the souls in her possession has been taking on her. Not only has she become more feeble and lost large patches of her hair, but the skin on her face is starting to come apart in tatters . She honestly seems to be hundreds of years old.

A loud bang rings out as Amos discharges his shotgun once more. Althea stops. She then looks in the direction of the sound momentarily and turns and scurries off into the woods. Lynn and Madeline can hear Amos running. And from the sound of it, he is headed in their direction.

"Open the car door!" he yells out.

Lynn runs and unlocks the door and pulls it open. She and Madeline then run to the other side of the car and start to jump in as Amos emerges from the back side of the gas station at a full gallop. Without missing a step, he runs full speed to the open car door and grabs a handful of shotgun shells from the box lying on the back seat.

As soon as he reloads the gun, a man appears from around the rear of the station. It is the same man that walked Madeline and Lynn to their car the first time they were in the forest. But this time, he is different. His eyes are bloodshot, and he is still wearing the same clothes that he wore then, except now, they are dirty and bedraggled.

He is walking as if he is in a trans-like state, dragging one of his legs as he moves. His shoes are worn clean through their soles, and his visible feet are blistered and bleeding. It is as if he has been walking around in those woods nonstop for heaven knows how long. Perhaps also searching for the item they removed from the den.

Lynn and Madeline flinch as Amos's shotgun rings out again. The impact from the blast knocks the festering remains of what once was a person clean past the far side of the car. And before he can stop his backward momentum, a second blast is delivered. This blast knocks him into the drainage ditch that lies between the gas station's lot and the road.

The three of them stand silently, looking off into the ditch at the remains. Lynn and Madeline struggle within themselves to find some trace of remorse or compassion for the soulless shell that lies before them. Even the thought of something like this happening just a year ago would have sent them both running and screaming. But now, they just stand there, treading in their inner feelings without showing any outward emotion.

After changing the tire, they load into the car and rush toward Jackson.

Chapter 27

A SURPRISE

As DUSK ONCE AGAIN BECOMES night, Lynn, Amos, and Madeline make their way onto the main road. With Madeline driving and Lynn sitting next to her, Amos asks, "Are you ladies all right up there?" The physical activities of the day start to take their toll on his elderly body.

"We're just fine up here. You can just sit back and relax," Lynn replies in a crisp and upbeat tone.

Mumbling something in response, he dozes off to sleep.

With the sound of Amos's snoring serenading them, Lynn and Madeline keep a keen eye on the road as the fog rolls its way into the low-lying areas.

"It's amazing how peaceful things look out there, isn't it?" says Lynn.

Madeline replies, "Sure is. But you know what? If by some small favor of God, we're able to get through this, I will never take my son David for granted again. If nothing else, this whole ordeal has taught me that life can't be taken for granted, not even one second.

"My boys, and I have had a good and blessed life. And even with all of the issues that their father and I had, it all now seems for not. It's almost funny because, before their father died, one of my biggest worries was how we looked in the eyes of our boys.

"It had gotten to the point that I was willing to do almost anything to save that image. Even try and erase the fact that that man had cheated on me from almost day one of our long and turbulent marriage. Do you think that was wrong of me?"

Lynn replies, "We all have things in our past. Some might question why we hold them so dear to ourselves. But, if someone is judging you on what your heart is telling you to do or feel, that is probably not a person you would want to listen to anyway. And therefore, I for one wouldn't pay them much mind."

Once they arrive back in front of the hospital, Lynn asks Madeline to pull the car over across the street in front of the park so that they can hide the jars in a place where they won't be found. After helping Madeline and Lynn remove the last bags from the trunk, Amos hops back into the car and takes off to find a place to park.

They each grab bags from the pile and scurry off into the park.

"Where are we going?" asks Madeline.

"Follow me. I know just the place to hide them," Lynn answers.

As they walk under the draping canopy and up to the large hole at the base of the gigantic weeping willow tree,

Lynn carefully looks over into the opening, being as cautious as possible for fear of rousing the enormous beehive that reside within.

She reaches in and places the first bag into the hole. As she reaches back for the next bag, she happens to look up and notices a rather large gray cat sitting up in the branches of the tree. The cat stares at her and then jumps down out of the tree and runs off.

"Did you see that?" asks Lynn.

"See what?" asks Madeline.

"The cat that just jumped out of the tree and ran off into the park…Never mind! Pass me another one of those bags so that we can hurry up and get the hell out of here," Lynn replies.

After hiding the last of the jars, they head back down the path that leads out of the park, where shortly afterward, they are joined by Amos. They all then head toward the hospital. Although no one says anything, they all feel an eerie stillness in the air.

As they wait on an oncoming car to pass before crossing the street, another cat darts out from seemingly nowhere, causing the vehicle screech to a halt . The cat stops and bares its sharp teeth as it squats and makes a hissing sound. It then runs off and disappears into the underbrush in the park.

Although they only see the cat momentarily, they are almost sure that it is the same cat that the old woman called Mama cat. That could just mean one thing, Lynn and Madeline think to themselves: Not only is Althea on her way there, but Ms. Irma is somewhere about as well.

"Why don't you ladies go on into the hospital and check on David and Willie, and I'll head back to the car? I was lucky and got a parking space where I can see the whole front of the hospital. I'll be in the car with my shotgun, keeping an eye on things," Amos says.

After thanking him once more for coming with them, Lynn and Madeline walk into the hospital. Once inside, the only other person that they see, is a receptionist sitting at the desk near the entrance. The hallways and waiting areas are empty.

The absents of all the daytime hustle and seemingly endless activity has been replaced with a quiet and uneasy emptiness. Lynn hustles off toward Willie's room, and Madeline does the same toward David's room.

Lynn walks off the elevator and turns down the hall toward the nurse's station. As she walks up to the station, she doesn't see anyone there. After waiting for a minute or so, she walks down the hall toward Willie's ward.

"Hello! Hello! Nurse!" she calls out as she slowly walks down the hall.

As she walks up to the door, she looks through its glass window. The room is dark, except for the light shining through the glass. The bright light from the hall projects the row of patient-filled beds onto the wall on the other side of the room, just like before. Lynn slowly rotates the doorknob and pushes the door open, only wide enough for her to enter.

She then starts to walk across the room toward Willie's bed. But the closer she gets, the more it looks like there is movement underneath the blanket that covers whomever it is lying in Willie's bed. Willie can't move, Lynn thinks, which means that he must've passed away. The hospital must've placed another patient in his bed .

She closes her eyes as she steps up to the bed. After asking God for strength, she looks down upon the blanket-covered figure lying in Willie's bed. Although the room is dark, with only the light from the small pane of glass in the door, her heart flutters, and tears immediately start to flow as wails of joy rush from her lips.

It is Willie who is in bed. And as he moans and turns in his restless sleep, Lynn eases down into the chair next to his bed and starts to pray. She dares not touch him for fear of him waking up and returning to his motionless condition.

She gets up and walks over to the door and looks out at the nurse's station and sees that no one has returned. She then walks back over to Willie's bed and sits back down in the chair. After many prayers of thanks, the minutes become hours, and the end of a long day comes calling. Lynn drifts off to sleep.

Chapter 28

SOME HONEY

WHILE SLEEPING, LYNN FINDS HERSELF in the middle of a horrible storm. The wind is blowing so hard that she can barely stay on her feet. She watches as the carriage—which she and the stranger once romantically rode in—is getting blown across the endless field where they sat, sipping wine in a warm breeze. The carriage smashes against the large willow tree where they sat while passionately caressing one another.

In this dream, she sees the water from the heated pool—where she once beckoned for the stranger's loving touch—get sucked up into a funnel-like whirlwind and then disperse all over the opened field. After making her way over to the willow tree, she clings to its trunk.

Off in a not-so-distant part of the field, she sees the muscular stranger making his way through the turbulent wind, heading in her direction. As he struggles with the strong winds, he waves his arms in the air as if he is trying to get her attention. Lynn calls out to him, but the constant howling of the wind drowns out her cries.

As he gets closer, she notices that his face is no longer blurred. And she can now make out his distinct facial features. She looks at the bridge of his nose, the color of his eyes, the taper and thickness of his eyebrows, she gasps, "Willie. It's you!"

"Yes, it's me. And you got to wake up, *now*!" he screams as he finally makes it to her.

Lynn opens her eyes to find Althea standing there with Uncle Leroy, the pistol that she took from her jacket pocket back when they were down in her den. And it is pointed at Willie's head.

Lynn slowly stands up and steps away from the chair.

"I know what it is that you want. Please! Just free Willie and David, and we will give you back the rest of the stuff," Lynn says.

"No!" shouts Althea. "You will give me all of them. And I just might let Willie and David rest in peace."

"You *bitch*! You think you are running something here? Don't try to play stupid, or I will blow his damn brains out all over this fucking room!" Althea snarls as she cocks the hammer of the pistol back.

Lynn slowly walks between Althea and Willie so that the gun is now pointed at her, instead of Willie. As she repositions herself, the light from the hall no longer halos around Althea's head and body, and she is able to better see her. Althea had grown so weak that, even with the assistance of her cane, she can hardly stand.

Although she wears a scarf over her head, slightly draped over part of her face, Lynn can see that her eyes are entirely covered with cataracts. Her voice is frail, and her breathing sounds raspy.

"What have you done with my souls?" she moans, keeping her distance from Lynn and repositioning herself so that she can continue to point the pistol at Willie's head.

"We don't have the jars!" Lynn says as she once more positions herself between the pistol and Willie. Althea repositions herself around Lynn once more and raises her arm to take aim.

"*Stop*!" shouts Lynn. "I meant to say that we don't have the jars here. But they are close by! And if you let Willie live, I will take you to them."

"If you are lying to me, I am going to make not only Willie but you and your children suffer in ways that Satan himself hasn't dreamed of," she says with a feeble smirk on her face. "Take me to them *now*!" she demands.

Lynn bends down, kisses Willie on the lips, and whispers, "I am so happy to have you. Love of my life." And as Lynn and Althea walk toward the door, Willie's eyes open, ever so slightly.

Lynn opens the door and steps into the hallway as Althea walks behind her with the pistol pointed at her back.

"Slow down, bitch!" Althea orders as she struggles to keep up. "Not so fast or I will fill your ass full of holes!" she says as she pulls her scarf down to further cover her disfigured facial feathers.

Lynn and Althea exit the hospital and walk into the park toward the large tree where the jars are hidden. The park is dark, with only the light from the stars and the moon to light the way. Once they are at the tree, Lynn points to the large opening.

"They are in there," she says.

As they walk under the tree's huge umbrella, what little light they had is now greatly diminished.

"In where?" Althea asks as she leans forward to look down into the opening. "I don't see anything in there, you lying bitch!"

Lynn steps toward the opening as if she is about to look in. "They are right there!" she says as she pushes Althea in . As Althea tumbles forward, the pistol discharges. The bullet knocks a large hole in the bottom of the hive.

As a massive stream of honey starts to flow onto Althea, she fires the pistol again and again in Lynn's direction, struggling to get back on her feet. The loud noise from the firing of the gun only further agitates the already angry bees, and they start to swarm and cover Althea's body.

She screams and swings her arm as if she is fighting an invisible man as Lynn ducks behind a nearby tree. Covered with honey and stinging bees, Althea runs toward the tree where Lynn is hiding. *Boom!* A gun discharge.

As the smoke clears, Althea lies on the ground, twitching, half of her head missing. Amos stands nearby with his shotgun still pointed in her direction.

"Now, who is the bitch?" he says as he lowers his gun.

Amos and Lynn stand there and watch as an endless number of bees pours out of the hive and onto Althea's body until it is completely covered. Then in one sudden swoosh, they all return to the colony. Leaving no evidence that Althea was ever there.

Chapter 29

THE THANKS

THE RAYS FROM THE SUN stretch out across the tree tops, creating a crowning effect that reaches high into the morning sky. A sparkling blanket of frost coats the entire landscape while the heat from the lake creates a scattered mist that partly covers it and its surrounding shores. Lynn, Howard, the children, and Amos all accompany Willie as he's pushed through the doors of the hospital toward a waiting car.

After thanking the nurse that pushed Willie to the car, Lynn turns back toward the car and sees a carriage coming from the park toward them. With its curtains drawn and the blinds tightly shut. The carriage stops in front of Lynn, and the door opens.

Its insides are dark with a sepulcher-like air about it. As Lynn looks in, its inner shadows reveal a thirty something years-younger Ms. Irma. She is sitting there with a young Mama cat on her lap. The sacks containing the jars are scattered about the seats and floor.

"I inspected the jars, and it looks as if all of them are accounted for. It even smells like we might have an extra one. Good! Maybe it was something else the caused Willie and David to be like they were?" Ms. Irma says as she stares at Willie sitting in the wheelchair.

Amos grips the shotgun lying in the back seat of the car, but Lynn replies , "Sure! Maybe you're right. They might have just had a nasty cold or something."

Ms. Irma looks down at the shotgun and then closes the door of the carriage, and it heads back into the park. Lynn then reaches down into her pocket and pulls out the dented lighter, an old wedding ring, and the small empty bottle that once contained the bullets removed from Amos's father's body.

A sizable fluffy snowflake lands on the back of Lynn's neck as she bends down to help Willie from the wheelchair and into the car. She wipes the cold, wet snowflake from her neck and is reminded that the fall of the year has ended and the winter has begun.

Before getting into the car, Lynn gazes out at the lake once more. And right before her eyes, walking through the scattered mist, a pair of ghostly figures appears. The two figures walk out to the edge for the mystic haze and pause as they slightly bow their heads as if to say thanks.

And at that moment, in her heart of hearts, she knows who they are. They are Thomas and his beloved Irene. They stand there, holding hands just like Lynn had imagined back when her grandmother had told her the story about seeing them in the pasture so many years ago. And as a light gust of wind blows through the mist, they dissipate into thin air.

A few months later, while reading the newspaper, Lynn sees an article about the police searching for someone who stole several bodies from an old cemetery. As she is reading the articles, Willie gets a call from the hospital. The doctor informs him of three more patients with symptoms similar to his. They are wondering if he would come by and let them run some more test on him.

Willie asks, "Who are they?"

The doctor replies, "A policeman, one of the hospital workers, and the doctor that worked with him..."

THE END

So...IF YOU EVER DECIDE TO go and take a little trip down south during autumn, and if while on that trip, you find yourself alone at night, driving the dark backroads. Please! Stay alert.

And if the night air that surrounds you has the brisk and deliberate frigidness of an early winter's chill, for heaven's sake, keep warm. If the numerous trees that adorn the ever so curvy roads have ornamented themselves in the bright fall shades of reds, oranges, and yellows, creating a spectacular and colorful view during the day and a brisk shadow dance in the bright moonlight—by all means, admire!

However, if during such time in your journey, you look around and find that you are in the part of the south known as the Delta, take heed! For that flicker in the night that we so easily ignore—or often write off as fictitious images of our imagination—might be something more than that anomaly or illusion. For the beings of the night may very well be afoot!

And I also want to warn the lustful giver, *beware*! For a gift that is not given from the heart may very well be the heart. When the receiver is a Merchant of Souls.

EARL LYNN'S STORIES ARE INSPIRED by many long hot days during the 1960's spent keeping his grandmother company in her small southern hometown. The middle child of eleven, Earl was allowed to spend the summers with his grandmother and her uncle Elijah, who was in his mid-eighties. Earl was greatly fascinated by the stories his great uncle would tell he about how things were when he was growing up in the south. Sometimes Earl played on the floor of his grandmother's bedroom as she talked on the phone with friends and relatives, and couldn't help but overhear about the singular things that were happening during that time. When he grew up and joined the military, he took to writing short stories in longhand to help fill the long and tedious idle periods.